Ruby's Personal Rainbow

And Other Stories

John Corral

ISBN-13: 9798826311011
ISBN-10: 1477123456

Cover design by: Art Painter
Library of Congress Control Number: 2018675309
Printed in the United States of America

For Tanya

"Short stories are tiny windows into other worlds and other minds and other dreams. They are journeys you can make to the far side of the universe and still be back in time for dinner."
--Neil Gaiman

CONTENTS

Title Page

Copyright

Dedication

Epigraph

Introduction

Ruby's Personal Rainbow 1

The Flawed Wisdom of John Wooden 10

The Plan 33

Pirate 35

A Final Portrait Of A Daughter 56

Poetic Love and License 58

A Barista Named Astrid 85

Margie 87

Saying Goodbye 96

About The Author 97

INTRODUCTION

This is a collection of short stories with snippets of life, introducing you to characters that will take you inside their hearts and souls to help you learn a little something about yourself. Four of these stories appeared in online publications from 2009 to 2016. They are supplemented by the title story, Ruby's Personal Rainbow, which is newly written for this book, and four very short pieces: The Plan, A Final Portrait of a Daughter, A Barista Named Astrid, and Saying Goodbye.

RUBY'S PERSONAL RAINBOW

Dr. Weissman told me that I loved too much. And he wasn't the first person who said that. All my friends said it. So did my sisters, my brother, my aunts. Hell, even my father said something like that. 'Ruby, you are a man junkie.' So it must be true.

But being in love with Mickie, my husband, was different than loving Jaimie, my son. With Mickie, love was being in pain, horrible pain that I felt deep in my gut. I tried loving him with everything I had. And yet he treated me like shit sometimes. I forgave him for that, excusing what he did, his moods, his bad temper, his put-downs, and his neglect. I even justified his hitting me. I told myself he had problems growing up, and that's why he would do bad things to me.

The night was black and hot with high summer, and the cicadas along the river were screaming as if they knew what was about to happen. Ruby had to turn on the radio to drown out their cries, but still, the music wasn't enough; they were too loud, so she snapped it back off in frustration.

Then she was glad to be aggravated by such a thing as screaming night bugs; lately, she had been moving through life like a ghost, in such a daze that she barely noticed if it was day or night or if she had even combed her hair.

I figured I was to blame for what Mickie did. I could have helped him to be better. That self-help book I bought him showed him how to change. I should have made him read it. But I didn't.

And I could have been better for him in other ways. I could have been more kind, more understanding, maybe even better looking for him. He wouldn't have gone out and found others to spend time with. I even forgave him for that.

Why did she hear everything so acutely now? Maybe the notion of getting Jaimie back was already opening her up actually to hear and see and taste again. She felt as if she were coming awake, the way a tree must feel when its leaves bud out just enough to drink the spring air.

Maybe she'd be able to feel something besides hurt for the first time since her baby had been taken away from her three months ago.

But Jaimie, my love for him, that's different. He's my baby. He's eleven but small for his age, something I've always been glad about since that made me feel I'd be able to keep him closer to me a little longer.

And Jaimie has never done anything but love me back, no matter what I did wrong. Even what I did to his father. I called Jamie my rainbow, my personal rainbow.

Up ahead was Ruby's mother-in-law Minnie's driveway. Ex-mother-in-law, although Ruby could hardly think of her that way. Minnie had been like a mother to her for the past six years. The mother she'd never had. But the fact of the matter was that Minnie was Mickie's mother, so she had to be the enemy now, as crazy as that seemed.

Ruby sniffed and shook her head at this; things sometimes didn't make sense. Things didn't have to be this complicated, this hard. But that's the way Mickie had made everything.

As she turned into Minnie's driveway, Ruby clicked off her headlights, and her eyes adjusted as if being tuned by a little shiny knob. The night wasn't so dark after all since the moon had drifted out from behind the black mountain, and she could see well enough to roll right on down the steep driveway with ease, so she notched the gearshift up into neutral and turned off the ignition too.

Immediately she realized that the cicadas had silenced entirely, which seemed especially strange since Minnie's house was tucked into a bend of the river, where she'd expect them to be even louder. When finally the car came to a stop near Minnie's front porch—the long tendrils of the willows brushing to a whispery stop against the car's hood—the world seemed a tranquil place.

Ruby sat there for a short time and could hear the tambourine shake of the cicadas back up the river, but they were quiet here, so quiet that she was surprised to hear the lonesome call of a whip-poor-will who sat close by, watching.

Most people she knew thought a whip-poor-will's call was lonesome, even frightening. Some people said a whip-poor-will announced death at hand. But others saw it as a sign of luck. She had always liked the mystery of thinking the bird might be a death omen, but tonight she chose to think of it as lucky. Sometimes you had to fool yourself into believing the thing that would get you through.

Ruby got out, eased the car door shut, then leaned back in and plucked the pistol in the console between the seats. She weighed the cold, shiny gun on her palm and let out a jagged breath. "Lord have mercy," she said aloud. She talked to herself a lot these days, it seemed like.

But then she just sucked everything up, all her guilt and fear, and she marched with determination toward the house. She kept her eye on the front door, thought the way a soldier might about maneuvering up the sidewalk and across the gray painted boards of the porch and to the door.

Ruby tried not to notice Minnie's pretty geraniums and the chimes that hang from the eaves, making no sound in the still summer night. Seeing these things would remind her of Minnie's good, freckled hands digging into the potting soil, of Minnie looking up at her with a smile.

Ruby couldn't think of Minnie as a person right now because she didn't know what it would take to get her child back. But she had already decided she would do whatever it took.

She banged on the door hard, so hard that her knuckles smarted—three sharp raps.

She counted to three and knocked again, harder. Three strikes of her flat hand against the cool wood this time. Then her knuckles again, quicker and quicker, like jagged little rocks being thrown in quick succession. It was a warning, the sharp little taps, even though Minnie wouldn't be able to interpret them.

A bumbling attempt to open the door. The clatter of a door chain. The doorknob twisting. Then Minnie's face in the little crack where the chain held the door fastened.

"What is it?" Minnie said, her violet eyes peering over her glasses until they lit on Ruby's face. Curiosity, at first, then shock. "Ruby?"

"Let me have him, Minnie."

"Ruby, honey, you can't put me in the middle like this—"

"Let me have him, Minnie," Ruby repeated, each word a little holler, a puff of anger, and a mounting fury. "Right now!"

Minnie wanted to help her. She knew well that her son had lied and had used his crooked friends to help him gain custody of Jaimie. So she wanted to help; Ruby could see it in her eyes. But she couldn't. And Ruby knew she couldn't. She wasn't brave enough. "You know I can't—"

"You know what's right, now, Minnie," Ruby said, trying to measure her words and not get so upset that she couldn't speak. "You know there's not a reason in this world to take that child from me. You know Jaime belongs with his mother, with me. You know that in your heart. You know that because you're a mother."

"Ruby, don't—"

And then Ruby just let herself float outside her mind, and her heart and everything that she had known, and she kept repeating Jaimie's name in her mind.

Jaime, Jaime, Jaime, Jaime, Jaime, Jaime, Jaime Jaime.

My pretty, pretty boy. You're best thing that ever happened to me. You're the reason I live now. The only reason I go on with my life. You're my personal rainbow. My personal rainbow. My personal rainbow.

Jaime, Jaime, Jaime, Jaime, Jaime, Jaime, Jaime Jaime.

That was all she thought about. She let herself betaken away by determination, by what she knew she had to do.

Ruby stepped back and threw herself against the door with such force that the impact knocked Minnie away but did not break the chain. Minnie righted herself and came rushing back to shut the door, just as Ruby's shoulder hit it again. This time the little gold chain broke like a rubber band, and the door was flying open, and Ruby was in the house, Minnie's good, familiar place that always smelled like bacon grease and fresh coffee.

"Ruby, you've lost your mind, honey, you've—" Then Minnie was falling back, that surprised look of imbalance crossing her face just before she fell with all her weight across the coffee table.

There was a great clatter of breaking things. Little whatnots that crowded Minnie's living room. She had kept a big orange ashtray twenty years past her smoking husband's death. An iridescent candy dish that had belonged to Minnie's great granny. A hundred years old, at least. Ruby had once loved it, had once held it up to the sunlight, and watched the colors change within its curves.

Ruby realized that she had struck Minnie across the face with the butt of the gun. There was a gash beneath her eye, a thin line of blood popping out. Minnie put her hand up to it, then moaned, not because of the cut, it seemed, but because of the way she had hit the coffee table. It was all Ruby could do not to stop and help her mother-in-law up, to help her, but she reminded herself of what was more important.

Jaime, Jaime, Jaime, Jaime, Jaime, Jaime, Jaime Jaime.

She didn't allow herself to look back at Minnie. She pressed on. She had to be a mother. Sometimes you can't be a mother and a human being. You had to choose one over the other. Some people never knew what that was like, to have to make that choice, but she did. She had studied on it for the past three months, and this was what she would have to do. Her child had been taken from her, and she was by God taking him back.

Ruby moved down the hallway, and the house seemed to swirl around her, shifting and turning to confuse her.

"Jaimie?" she called. "Jaimie, baby? Where you at, baby?"

So many framed photographs on the hallway wall. Mickie in grade school, graduating high school, with a big buck he'd shot, with a basketball trophy. Mickie graduating college.

Further on, Mickie and Ruby's wedding picture. Mickie and Ruby at Cumberland Falls. Mickie and Ruby dressed up like Bonnie and Clyde in a sepia-toned photo taken at Dollywood. Baby pictures of

Jaimie.

Too many pictures, all those lies told for the camera. Too many memories, all of them in old cheap plastic frames, although Minnie had plenty of money. They seemed to rock and twist on the wall, becoming one big moving picture that caused Ruby to get dizzy and want to throw up.

Jaime, Jaime, Jaime, Jaime, Jaime, Jaime, Jaime Jaime.

"Jaimie!"

All at once, she was aware of a television playing the closing music to The Tonight Show. She moved like a hunter, the pistol out in front of her. She started at this realization, stopped, and shoved the gun into the waistband of her Levis, around in the back where Jaimie wouldn't see it.

"Jaimie?" She was cooing now, her mother voice, the voice that knows a child is asleep but still calls out for him.

There he lay in the blue glow of the television, that eerie light that flickered around the room. He had been snuggled up to Minnie, who always sat up late and ate Almond Joys in bed while she watched talk shows or the late movie.

Jaimie hadn't awakened when Minnie had left him there to answer the door. He was on his back, one arm above his head, the other resting on his chest with a tightened fist. The way he always slept.

Ruby hadn't laid eyes on her child in three months. She had the momentary urge to just stretch out beside him, pull him into her, and let his mouth rest warm and breathe against her neck. It would be so good—the best thing in her life, ever—to stretch out and just go to sleep. She was so exhausted, so tired. She didn't know if she could make it.

Jaime, Jaime, Jaime, Jaime, Jaime, Jaime, Jaime Jaime.

But she couldn't lie down. She grabbed him up and rushed back toward the front of the house, catching glimpses of all those photographs. She tried not to look at Minnie, who still lay in the broken wood and glass of the coffee table, moaning Ruby's name, begging for help.

Minnie started to stir harder when she saw Ruby moving down the hallway. She reached out her arm; her face was so full of hurt and worry. Not anger. Not even malice. But hurt, her feelings hurt to the bone, far worse than any hurt she felt to her body. A face that Ruby would never forget.

"Please don't do this," Minnie called as if begging for her life. But Ruby did not hear her.

Jaime, Jaime, Jaime, Jaime, Jaime, Jaime, Jaime Jaime.

Ruby shifted Jaimie on her hip, pulled him closer, and rushed on out, not wanting to leave Minnie this way. But she had to; there was no choice. This was how far she would go for him.

She ran to the car and slid him onto the seat. A turn of the key, the slide of the gear, a stomp of the accelerator, and then she was peeling out, gravel pinging onto the porch. As she drove away, the wisps of the willow sucked away as the car bounced up the driveway and onto the road, back onto the smooth purr of blacktop.

Ruby breathed hard. It was done. She had her child again. She didn't remember the last time she had been so happy. Was it the day she married Mickie? No, this felt much better. Nothing was better than to be with the love of her life, her baby, her Jaimie. The cicadas screamed alongside the black river in the hot, still night of a dog's summer as if they were ecstatic too. Ruby drove off. There was only one thing on her mind.

Jaime, Jaime, Jaime, Jaime, Jaime, Jaime, Jaime Jaime.

My pretty, pretty boy. You're best thing that ever happened to me. You're the reason I live now. The only reason I go on with my life. You're my personal rainbow. My personal rainbow. My personal rainbow.

THE FLAWED WISDOM OF JOHN WOODEN

Those who guard their lips preserve their lives, but those who speak rashly will come to ruin. —Proverbs 13:3

When you're sure you're right, let everyone know it. Have courage in your convictions, and don't be deterred by forces that expect you to bend to their will. —John Wooden

I am a God-fearing man who was taught by my father all there was to know about life through verses from the Bible. And I am also a high school basketball coach who used quotes from John Wooden, arguably the greatest college basketball coach of all time, as the blueprint for my success as a coach. Yet, I think Coach Wooden has let me down by following his advice too closely.

That happened one night in a game at the Blaine, Idaho, gym. My team, the Blaine Bobcats, was ahead by two points, and with only 22 seconds left on the clock, a player from the other team shot the ball. I saw the ball spinning high above the rim, and I wondered if it wasn't going into orbit because it was so high. When it did come twirling out of the air, it hit the front of the rim and went flying upward once again.

At that point, Lance Philby, my only star, leaped and tipped the ball to one of the Spartans standing underneath the basket. In his haste to make it right, he reached out and slapped at the ball, missing the other player's hand by a good three or four inches. At least that's how I saw it.

Unfortunately, the ref saw it differently, as did everyone else sitting in the stands. He blew his whistle with a long shrieking trill, and I had no choice but to come flying off the bench and fight for what I thought was best for my team. "You better start making the right calls, Mathews, or we'll be talking about it in the parking lot after the game."

"I will get you for that one," Mathews screamed, again blowing his whistle.

Mathews was Mathews, my nemesis from birth. We'd come out of our mothers' wombs vowing to take the other down. Our first quarrel came when we were only fourteen years old. We were playing marbles, and I swore I saw him slip one of my favorite steelies into his pocket, though he pretended otherwise. After a long verbal blast, I wrestled him to the ground, and despite his wide girth and a good thirty-five pounds on me, I let fly with both hands and bloodied his nose.

That evening my father, a hard slip of a man, sat me down and asked, "Were you right? Did he steal? You had every right to do what you did if he did."

The kid that Lane had fouled stepped to the line and let go with four free throws, two for Lane's supposed misstep and two more for my threat to pummel Mathews in the parking lot. Each one lifted into the air with the ease of a butterfly and found their way into the basket, putting their team up by two points, with only seconds left on the time clock.

"Let that be a lesson to you," Mathews shouted from the foul line.

I wiped the sweat off my brow and thought about the terribleness he had put me through and the fact that we couldn't agree about anything, beat-up Chevys, girls in the parking lot, all driven home by the time I saw him walking down the street hand in hand with his mother. I picked up a rock and aimed it directly at the back of his head. Luckily, it veered to the left and tumbled into the street.

I tried settling back into the game, but my mind was elsewhere. Mitchell, my water boy, nudged me in the side and suggested I calm down. But the next time down the court, Mathews gave me a dirty look, and I slipped over the line. "You know, having you was your mother's biggest mistake," I yelled.

Mathews's face flashed from red to white, and by now, the score meant nothing to me. I despised every inch of his broad, heavy jowls, not to mention his lumbering gait up and down the court.

"I'm running you to the showers for that one," he said from center court.

I never did know what came over me, but an impulse took control, and I figured public shaming was my only recourse. I let loose with a series of dance steps, something I usually reserved for the privacy of my own home. But reducing Mathews to nothing more than a pile of ridicule was my only desire.

"Get off the court!" Mathews shouted, "Or I'll hit you with another technical!"

I wiggled my hips and held my hands in the air like I had an imaginary dance partner. I was a Cuban fireball in the making. I spun and twirled and aimed my rear end right at Mathews as if to say there was no difference between the two.

Mathews's mouth gaped open and closed, and I declared myself a winner. By now, everyone in the Blaine gym, parents and students, Spartans and otherwise, were standing up and applauding my every move. I had no choice but to bow to the uproarious crowd like I was hailing the end of a Broadway play.

Turning, I had one place in mind, the dark dang basement, otherwise known as a locker room. But before I could disappear, I had to face my biggest challenge of the evening, my wife, Margie, a teacher of grades one through three.

She was sitting high in the stands, staring directly at me over the long rows. Her face was delicate and white as if carved out of ivory. I offered up only a glimpse before disappearing into the locker room. After all, I knew what she was thinking. Downstairs, I sat and stared at a cold cement floor. Not far away was a chalkboard that read "Beat the Spartans."

△△△

Driving home, I was lost in a swirl that got the best of me. The frosty fields and long vistas barely drew my attention. Our farmhouse looked lonely and out of place. My wife had parked the family car near the back door, closer to the porch than she had ever done before. I parked my beat-up truck right alongside.

The only light was a soft glow emanating from the living room. I thought for sure Margie would be sitting at the kitchen table, staring out the far window. Instead, the bedroom door was closed, and for a moment, I thought the couch was my only option, but that might have made her mad, and I'd probably done enough damage for one evening.

Opening the door, I saw Margie sleeping slightly curled up and with both hands clinging to her pillow. Naked, I slipped beneath the sheets, still humming with thoughts of what I had done to my team. Scooting even closer, I thought of nuzzling her shoulders or kissing her on the neck, but breaking her silence would have violated the code that defined us.

We reconvened in the kitchen in the morning, me on one side, her on the other. "Mathews really gave it to us again, didn't he?"

"Are you sure about that?"

"Everyone knows he has it in for me, always has."

"But everyone thinks he made the right call."

"Not from where I was sitting. I swear Lane never even came close to touching him."

"But telling him he should have never been born, wouldn't you say that was a bit much?"

"The guy irks me; that's all I can say. Besides, how are we supposed to win a state championship with him in the way?"

"Is a trophy that important?"

"It is for me. I want to be the first coach in the school's history to bring home the big prize."

"But do you have to be a maniac in the process? What if I taught my classes like that?"

"Last place is very unappealing."

"So is having to learn how to shoot a free throw in the middle of the supermarket."

She was referring to another day when I was off the mark. My team was missing free throws, and that's all I had on my mind. One day in the grocery store, I suggested Margie practice lofting a loaf of bread into a shopping cart from seven feet away. "Everything is in the follow-through. You have to dream it into the basket." Needless to say, she declined.

She leveled a look at me. "But what about other things, like going for a drive, having your family over for dinner, or even taking a ride to Twin Falls?"

I wanted to say we had a farm to groom and a group of boys who couldn't shoot straight, but I knew divorce was trilling through her mind, and I didn't want to push her any more than I already had.

"Maybe you should leave the rumba to those who know how to do it," she said.

Later that day, the phone rang. I had a feeling it was for me, and sure enough, it was.

"Good morning, this is Principal Withers. I think we need to talk."

"On a Saturday?"

"I hate waiting around. How about coming in and hearing what I have to say."

"Can I feed my cows first?"

"Sure. How does noon sound?"

△△△

Noon would give me time to rehearse my apology and possibly save my season. I pulled up to the high school and saw Withers's black sedan sitting not far away. Other than that, the lot was empty. Students were home like they were supposed to be, tending to their chores. Playing out in the background of all our lives was the threat of Hitler marching through Europe, and none of us knew what to think.

Inside the modest construction of brick and mortar, I looked around. Not long ago, these hallways were my home, me a smallish forward with a slashing style and an eye for the basket. Close by was a trophy case with seven or eight statements of victory sitting on the other side of the shiny glass.

One of those victories belonged to me and the class of '31, the year we brought home a conference championship, only to lose to a bigger and faster team from Boise in the finals. I envisioned one more trophy idling in the case that my Bobcats and the whole town of Blaine could enjoy.

At the end of the hallway, I saw Withers's office was closed. The only sign of life was a bar of light running across the bottom of the door. Knocking, I waited for a reply and then stepped inside. Withers was sitting at a small desk with a typewriter off to the side.

He was a thick man with a foreboding presence. He and a staff of three oversaw the lives of thirty-seven students and six or seven teachers, of which I wasn't one. My only job was to coach, and coach to win.

"Thanks for coming in on such short notice. I thought it best to settle this matter before the whole town is in an uproar."

"I didn't know they were."

"My phone's been ringing nonstop. You put on quite a show."

"We all know that Mathews and I have never gotten along."

"But telling a man, he should have never been born. I would say that's pretty severe, wouldn't you?"

"The heat of the moment, I guess."

He fell into a diatribe about manners and morality, and I listened the best I could. "I've been on the phone with the superintendent. We're going to sit you down for five games without pay. It's either that or face a revolt from many parents."

"Was I that bad?"

"We don't like a lot of commotion. We're a quiet people here in Blaine."

"But who's going to coach the boys?"

"Mitchell can do it. I hear he's a smart little lad."

"But he's the water boy."

"Maybe he'll keep his cool."

ΔΔΔ

Going home was my only thought, but why? So I could spend more time with Margie staring at me like I was a ghost? Besides, I needed to bring my father into the loop. If not, I'd hear about it in a big way.

Everyone called him Larry, but I went with Dad, and then only when it was necessary. A house painter by trade, he kept Blaine High shiny and bright. He'd throw me a firm but hardly friendly nod when we passed in the hallways.

I knocked on his door and waited for an answer. Most likely, he was reading his morning paper and dousing himself with a few beers. He never drank to excess, just enough to maintain a steady hum throughout the day.

"Ah, it's the showman."

"So you heard?"

"Who hasn't?"

"I didn't think I was that bad."

"I hear Mrs. Mathews took to her bed."

"I can't help it if her son acts like he's nearly blind."

"The Spartans are sure happy that he is."

"We'll get them next time if there is one. Withers just sat me down for five games."

"I'm assuming you came to borrow some money?"

"Most likely, we'll have to dip into our savings. If not, I'll find something on the side."

I couldn't help but survey the room. The only thing calling to me was a photo of my mother on the mantel. She was dressed in white, and the picture was taken only days before she was slain by a burrowing set of pathogens, otherwise known as the flu epidemic of 1918.

After a mercy mission to Salt Lake City to help her befallen sister, my mother came home and took to her bed. On day three, my father called the doctor. A short, wiry man, the doc came right over, but her lungs were filling with fluid, and she was flirting with a fever of 103.

On a Sunday, he came back for a second visit. After tending to her for nearly an hour, he emerged from her room and stared at the floor. "She's gone," he whispered, barely loud enough for me to hear.

With that, my father drove his fist into the wall. The loud smack did little but drive my seven-year-old body into the corner of the room. His echoing cry of "Goddammit to hell" floated over me like a blast of heat before settling into me and overtaking my pores and permanently sealing me into place.

"Do you think much about her?" I asked, pointing at the photo.

"I've gone numb doing that very thing."

"What do you think she would have thought of my shenanigans?"

"She was gentle in ways I never understood, like Margie is."

"That's what everyone says."

"They have a softness you don't always see around here."

ΔΔΔ

Driving home, I revved up my thoughts about money. If sliding into our savings was too troubling a thought, I'd offer to paint houses. After all, I'd heard my father going on about brushes and how to cover a wall in smooth, even strokes many a time. What I couldn't do was sit at the kitchen table and draw up plays without a team to perform them.

To my surprise, I saw Margie's father, Horatio Summers, standing in the driveway. Not far away was his brand-new Lincoln, a 1940 Town Car. A Supreme Court judge by day and a controlling father by night, he nodded when I stepped out of my car.

"Margie called me last night. We think it's best if she comes home for a while. Until you've had time to sort out your priorities."

"I'm paid to win championships."

"But at what cost?"

"The cost that comes with not finishing in third place."

Inside, Margie was sitting at the kitchen table. Her face was serene but not very far from worry. Next to her on the floor was her suitcase. The one I'd bought for her when we first made the trek from Reno to Idaho.

"I'll come back when you calm down a bit. I was nearly sick to my stomach last night after the game."

"But what about school? Who's going to teach the kids?"

"I just got off the phone with Withers. He said he'd make arrangements."

"He's set me down for five games."

"I know, he told me."

"What's that tell us about decorum?" Horatio said, patting his daughter on the shoulder.

"I crossed a line. But do we need to go this far? I'll see to it that it won't happen again."

"We've always respected all you've done for Margie. There's no question you've provided wonderfully for her, but it's the obsessiveness we worry about."

"I call it paying attention to details."

"I understand you're thinking of coaching your team through

the summer? Isn't that the time of year they should be playing baseball?"

"Rounding the bases never helped anyone shoot a free throw."

△△△

On day five of my lonely exile, I woke to a light layering of snow and coldness I hadn't experienced in more than a year. Sitting at the kitchen table, I learned from the radio that my Bobcats had fallen to the Jerome Tigers, 57 to 39. Most likely, Lance Philby had 37 of those points.

My only refuge was out back behind the barn, where the crows flew, and the cows bleated in the distance. A basket with a raggedy net was hanging from the side, not far from where I parked my pickup. It was there that I'd won many a game, darting with a lean look in my eye, each time scoring a point that propelled my imaginary team to victory.

Despite the darkening clouds and the hint of more snow on the way, I kept shooting. Some shots found their mark, and others didn't, but the ache in my inner thighs vanished after I made three in a row. Soon I was dashing and darting, convinced I could play again. If only my players had the same desire to win that I did. If so, we'd line the rafters with banners, and I would be the grandmaster of Blaine.

Shortly after nailing a free throw, I heard the phone ring. My first impulse was to ignore it. Explaining my love for the rumba was not my idea of fun. But by the third ring, I thought otherwise. Maybe it was Margie. Maybe being back in Reno wasn't the fun ride she thought it would be when she loaded her bags into the car and snuggled close to her father.

I tossed the ball aside and ran into the house. By the seventh ring, I had it. I heard a voice, but it wasn't Margie's.

"Hey, Coach, how've you been?"

Instantly I recognized Lane's voice. "I'm fine, putting in my time here."

"That's good."

"I understand the Tigers were a bit too much for you."

"They had more muscle under the basket than we did."

"How was Mitchell?"

"Let's say the water tasted good."

"Four more games, and I'll be back patrolling the sidelines once again."

"We're all rooting for you, but that's not why I'm calling. My father is wondering if you'd like to come work for him at his dance studio. He says you're a natural."

"I teach dance? That's impossible."

"He said not to worry about it. Besides, it comes with a paycheck."

I hung up the phone and thought about it. Living in solitude was not for me. Besides, I needed to earn some money. The following day, I was up early, standing in front of Mel's Wonderful World of Dance, a tall gray building not far from Blaine High.

I took a deep breath, did a two-step, and then opened the front door. Inside I saw the vast expanse of a dance floor. On three sides of the room were giant mirrors, all shiny and clean. Before I could take a step, Mel came running up to me. "Thank you so much for joining us. We're excited about having you on board."

"But I'm not sure I can be of much help."

"I saw you in action the other night. You practically glided across the floor."

"I've never given this any thought, but I teach my players how to tap."

"We know. Lane loves it."

"I tell them there are three rules for being on my team. Tap, listen, and do what you're told."

"We do think it's best if you audition first. We have to be careful who we throw to the wolves around here," he said. "Let me get Aubrey; she's more than thrilled about this."

A minute later, a tall blonde woman in a black leotard swept into the room. "We both think you're going to be a great addition to the staff."

"I tap all the time at home. I don't think I'll need any music."

"Let's see what you've got under the hood," Mel said, taking a step backward.

I slipped off my jacket and stretched my arms over my head. With only a count of three, I let go with a long flurry of steps. Tipiti-tipiti-tap. Tipiti-tipiti-tap. I found my timing with ease, and right after came that all-important glow. I could have tapped until my legs fell off.

Mel laughed and clapped his hands. "Simply marvelous. You're everything we've been looking for."

"And we're going to have a rumba special next week. Two for the price of one," Aubrey said.

"Are you sure you want me doing this? That's how I got in trouble in the first place.

"We will make you a star," Mel said, patting me on the back.

△△△

The following week, it was rumba, rumba, and rumba some more. Big and tall, sure-footed and wide, we didn't give a damn. The First

Annual Rumba Festival was a mind-bending success. It felt like half the town showed up for lessons. Mel, Aubrey, and I held forth with swirls and twirls for six long days, not to mention dips and dives. We didn't care if they were farmers, merchants, or down-in-the-dirt dropouts from Blaine High.

For seventeen dollars and thirty-five cents a head, we slithered and dithered until our legs ached, and our eyes glistened every time another dollar bill floated into the cash drawer and laid there like an Olympian who had crossed the finish line and won a gold medal.

Right before lunch, Mel came up to me and smiled. "Marcella Mathews is coming in today for what we hope is a series of lessons."

"Rob Mathews's sister?"

"The same."

"But we all know about the Mathews and me."

"We're not worried about that. Besides, Marcella is very nice. When's the last time you saw her?"

I ran through the dark corridors of my mind. "Been some time. Is she still running the farm out on the highway?"

"Damn near all by herself. She says she needs a break in the action. And besides, she was very excited to hear you'll be teaching her."

"But a Mathews?"

After finishing my sandwich, I saw her pulling up in a big hay truck with a dented front end and a faded right door. She hadn't changed much over the years. She is tall and lumbering, very much like her brother, with wide hips and thick, muscular legs.

"I couldn't believe it when Mel told me you would be giving me lessons."

"Well, I need to stay employed."

"I heard you and Rob put on quite a show."

"Seems to be what we do best."

"Somebody needs to pin his ears back now and then."

Mel yelled from across the room. "Nice to see you, Marcella. Let me get the music going."

"Have you ever rumbaed before?" I asked.

"Only in my dreams."

The warm, driving sound of a Latin band soon filled the room.

"Nice," Marcella said.

"Follow my lead, and you'll be fine."

I cupped my hand around Marcella's and lifted it into the air. I wrapped my other arm around her waist and pulled her a step closer, telling myself not to think about her brother. Our first step was awkward and out of sync, with the heavy beat hovering over me.

"Relax into me, if you can," I said.

She let her shoulders sink, and the touch of her hand on my shoulder softened. "This is so exciting."

"I like what I'm seeing," Mel said.

Marcella followed right along, slipping and sliding, letting her wide hips guide her across the floor, perfectly in line with the music.

"Way to go, Marcella. You're getting the hang of this," Mel yelled once again.

Diving deeper into the sounds, I saw the wet glint in her eye, and I fought the urge to hold her more tightly. Though Margie was still in Reno, she was very much on my mind.

"I think I was born to do this," Marcella said.

I let her words swim over the top of me, and in my mind's eye, I saw myself wearing a wide Panama hat and swaggering down the streets of Havana.

"Now, I want you to really let go through the hips and feel the music," I told her.

"I swear that saxophone player must be rolling in lava," Marcella said.

Both of us were dipping and sliding in perfect harmony to the music, and the more we danced, the more I yearned for the hard, driving pulse to never end.

Near the end of a luxurious piano solo, I let my arms swing out, and Marcella twirled with the ease of a ballerina. Shimmering from side to side, she stared at me with a warm glow in her eyes, and I never once let her escape the light grip of my fingertips.

"Bravo!" Mel screamed in a high-pitched voice.

The music ended with a long, soothing comedown that was baked at the right temperature. Marcella was breathing heavily, and her face was lined with sweat. "I think we flirted with ecstasy," she said.

Less than three feet away, I fought the need to feel the warmth of her body pressing into mine, and the thought of her willingness to ask for more caused my breathing to heave up and down in ways I found embarrassing. Who would have thought the secret of life was hiding inside the steamy beat of a saxophone from somewhere in South America.

△△△

On my way home, I thought only of Marcella. Could she indeed be the one I needed to be with for the rest of my life? And what would that be like, sitting with Mathews and his surrounding tribe? What were Marcella, he, and I supposed to talk about? The art of refereeing a game?

Glancing at the clock, I saw that suppertime was not far away. That meant Margie was buried inside a book while her mother tended to a plate of spaghetti in the kitchen.

I dialed a number that came quickly to me, Fairview 3-7476. In the middle of the third ring, the Judge answered.

"Hello, can I speak with Margie?"

A pause lingered on the line. "I don't think that's a good idea. She's having one of those days."

"What does that mean?"

"She's been resting. This ordeal has been hard on her."

"Are you saying she wants to come home?"

"I'm not saying anything of the kind. Why don't you call back in a few days?"

Hanging up, I thought maybe this was something we could work our way through. Me, the rebellious coach, her the tender surveyor of children.

Around nine, I heard the loud roar of a truck coming down the driveway. I hoped it wasn't one of my students wanting a long dissertation on the history of dance. Glancing outside, I saw Marcella finding her way across the front yard.

Suddenly my breath was fluttering, and I thought of turning off the lights and hiding. But by the third rap, I knew I had to answer the door.

Opening it only a few inches, I saw her face surrounded by a halo of light. "Next week was too far away," she said.

"Come in, come in."

She stepped into the kitchen and stared at the floor. "I think the music is still beating inside me."

"Is that a good thing?"

"I'm not sure, but I can't stop thinking about our lesson."

"I do think we shined it up a bit."

Marcella moistened her lips and stared right at me. "I might regret saying this, but I need to know if Margie is ever coming back."

"Let's say we're taking a time-out."

"But for how long? Days, weeks, years, what?"

"The rigors of coaching have taken their toll on us."

"But I have to say, I've seen the two of you at games. Neither of you ever looks very happy."

"I've been drawn to her since I met her."

"But round pegs and square holes. You know how that goes."

"One day, they might find their way."

Bear-like and ready, she wrapped her thick arms around me and squeezed until a warm flush flowed through the center of my body.

My first impulse was to break away and not get lost inside her. But the more I wiggled, the more I felt the brusque slide of her overalls across my clean white shirt, and I finally had what I was looking for, flesh to flesh, bone to bone, the mother lode in every way.

"Please don't let go of me," she said.

"But Marcella, I'm married."

"But I have visions of you tap-dancing on my chest."

Closing my eyes, I saw a long white valley, and it was like tumbling inside a cavern of nothingness, so I stepped backward. I wasn't ready to be so deep inside my own breath. "Not now, Marcella; it wouldn't be right."

She flexed and took a step back from my lingering body. "Oh, the music we could make."

I thought of Margie tucked away at her parents' home in Reno. "I need some water. I feel a headache coming on."

I closed my eyes and saw myself in an orchard with a bright shiny apple spinning just beyond my fingertips.

△△△

Later in the week, I sat in a room down the hallway from where Mel and Aubrey seemed to live most of the time. Over coffee, I thought of Marcella and our illustrious near miss. Some part of me needed another flash in the middle of the night. Another told me to stay away.

Mel scooted into the room and tapped his fingers on the table. "You've got a call. I'm not sure who it is."

Margie and her family came to mind. Walking into Mel's office, I cleared my throat and told myself not to sound desperate. "Hello."

"Principal Withers here. I'm wondering if we can't have a talk?"

"I'm listening."

"What do you think about coming back early?"

"I thought I was out for five games."

"We can't go zero and five; I'll have anarchy on my hands."

"But I have an obligation to Mel and Aubrey. We're in the middle of a rumba festival."

"Maybe you can do both. Tap by day, coach by night."

I held the phone in the cup of my hand and stared up at Mel. "They want me back."

"We knew this was coming. We'll have to work something out. Besides, Lane says the team is about to strangle Mitchell."

"Mr. Withers, tell the team I'm back in action."

△△△

I thought I would ebb between two worlds, but Mel and I came up with a plan to bring the team over to his studio for a day or two and let them dance away. That evening at five, my boys were standing in front of me. "From what I understand, we need to get our legs back. Without them, we don't stand a chance against Minico High."

I lined my boys up in an even row and motioned for Mel to turn on the music. Soon some big-band music filled the room. I glanced at Lane, and he gave me a smile that swept from one side of his face to the other. But there we were, eleven little warriors adorned in gym shorts and shiny black shoes with metal taps on their bottom.

I gave them one dazzling rat-a-tat-tat after another, yearning for us to be one large ensemble. Naturally, the smaller boys were right there with me, their little taps echoing with a steady beat. The bigger, more shabbily built boys struggled to keep up. Of course, Lane was a mountain stream in every way.

"That's it; listen to the hum. That's all there is to it; tap, and be willing to hear the song of life."

I closed my eyes, and one long tapping sound led to another. Soon I was swimming in a sustained rhythm of my own making. Suddenly the anguish of always wanting more out of Margie thinned down to a whispering vapor. Along with it went the farm, the need to win, and any lingering thoughts of Marcella.

Finally, I brought my tapping to a halt, but I jabbed my finger in the air and motioned for my team to keep going. Their young legs tapped with a sustaining pulse until the only thing that mattered was the loud booming sound that engulfed them.

"Now, let's finish with a flourish," I said, walking back and forth like the dance instructor I had become.

I quickly returned to my own brand of rat-a-tat-tat, but it was nothing more than a splash of dessert after a gourmet meal.

"Fellas, we're going to tap our way to victory."

ΔΔΔ

The next day, I opened the barn door and stared down at my livestock. Seven were cows, and five needed to be milked and readied for the day. Glancing out the window, I stared at our forty acres of productivity, nothing more than frozen soil waiting for the call of spring.

Later, I counted the rest of the day minute by minute. The past few weeks had been a spinout, an aberration of sorts. Soon Margie would be home, and the victories on the court would be piling up.

By late afternoon, I was in the locker room. I dispensed with the blackboard and any slogans about the Tigers being our only focus. Instead, I waited until everyone was dressed and ready to go.

Upstairs we could hear the band warming up. With it came the call of the dance studio, and I was almost ready to slip back into my other life.

"This is what we do. We play ball, and we play with a sense of freedom. That's all we need to know. We let the game come to us. The court is nothing more than a dance floor, and we're going to dance like no one has ever seen."

Mitchell lowered his head and mumbled what sounded like a prayer. Lane stood up and smacked his hands. "Let's show them what we got."

The boys slithered their way up the steps, with Lane in the lead. I chose to hold back until I heard the band strike up a long spark of music, and I followed soon after, making sure not to attract too much attention.

On the court, both teams ran through their layups. I folded my arms across my chest and looked around. Sitting in the bleachers, about ten rows up, was Margie. Next to her was her father, impassive and indifferent to the game's outcome. But she was eager for us to win. Gone was the tepid look that seemed to be so much a part of her. In its place was one of quiet reflection, the very one that drew me to her when we first met.

I waved and made sure the gesture was smooth and inviting. She smiled back at me, and I told myself not to make any assumptions but thought that maybe we could still be a happy farm couple with the team as the center point of our lives.

In the huddle, I caught sight of Marcella sitting high up in the stands, slumped forward with her arms resting across her thighs. Turning, I had to shake any thoughts of her away. "Let's play loose. Remember, we're here to have some fun," I shouted to my team.

Both teams wandered onto the court, lonesome boys with little thought of anything beyond what was right in front of them. Before tip-off, Mathews pulled up his pants and gave me a look that said he was up for more. In the parking lot, I'd pick him apart in little time. But I was beyond that now; dance had brought me to the hilltops, and that's where I wanted to stay.

"I'm so glad you're back," Mitchell whispered in my ear.

The Tigers controlled the ball with the tip, but I wasn't worried. We looked spry and springy in the legs. After their shot went up, we took possession and sprinted up the court.

The first pass, once we set up around the key, found its way to Lane, my slip-and-slide serpent of a player. Dribbling once, twice, he bled across the free-throw line, and three Tigers collapsed around him. He leaped with the pure grace of who he was, a by-product of Mel's Wonderful World of Dance.

He raised the ball above his head and let go at his peak. I watched it sail as if it were nothing more than a puff of air.

The ball hung there, arching high over the rim, seemingly for seconds. It descended without any players altering its flight. I saw it fall, and the shimmering whiteness of the net engulfed me. If my arms had been longer, I would have reached out and cradled that ball, maybe more than anything in my life.

We won that night. But more importantly, I learned that the wisdom of John Wooden had its limitations—at least for me.

THE PLAN

At the hideout, Mike went through the plan once again, for the hundredth time it seemed, and so we sat there bored.

Except for Arnie, who was talking, laughing, and cracking up. That was his way all the time. He never stopped clowning.

"Before you leave, check your cell phones," Mike said, "and make sure they're on. Keep them on vibrate, not ring."

Arnie made a face to show he was bored. He'd heard that before. We all had, on this job and several others.

Mike continued, "It's important to have them pressed against you somehow, in your hand and next to your face, if possible."

Another face from Arnie. He's a cut-up, and a born clown.

"Timing is everything on this one," Mike emphasized. "That is, if you want to get out alive."

We'd also heard that before from Mike, many times. Arnie made another face, a really crazy face.

Just then, outside, the wheelman's car arrived to pick us up. We went numb. Time for the caper. Time to get serious.

I checked my phone. It was a cheap model, bought in the market for a few dollars, because it was for a one time use.

Much later, only two of us sat together trying to make sense of what had happened.

When we found Arnie, soaking wet, and lifeless, he was still holding his phone, which was also lifeless.

"Next time, I'll get better phones," Mike finally said, "ones that work even in the rain.

PIRATE

He was dusty and bloody, more the former than the latter, and he had big ears, wiry hair, and a muzzle just beginning to grizzle. But his eyes were what caught my attention first, deep dark brown eyes, not pleading, but something else. A sort of quiet dignity, maybe even aloofness, as if he didn't need me or anyone of my kind being nice to him. That was it, an arrogance that declared he needed no one's pity.

He looked like the sort of dog that hadn't been taken care of and was looking to be rescued from that existence. Yes, I thought to myself, I can do that for you. I want to take you home and care for you. Why? I haven't a clue.

"He was dropped off while I was taking a break," said Pete, the vet technician at my animal hospital, who was on the stoop, smoking a cigarette, when it happened. "Dropped off like a sack of potatoes. I had to bring him in."

Pete had the dog in his arms—a mangy black-and-white mongrel —a Lab and something-else mix. Maybe shepherd or border collie. A gentle dog about two years old, mostly white but with a black tail and black patches, including one that encircles his left eye. The minute I laid eyes on the dog, I knew I'd call him Pirate.

I wasn't planning on adopting a dog. It's a joke among my wife, children, friends, and extended family. An animal doctor without family pets. The cobbler's family has no shoes. We'd had the occasional fish and hamster—none of which had survived very long in our household. But never a cat and never a dog.

The animal hospital's name is a bit of a joke for my line of work. Family Pet Care. Danny, my middle child, had thought up the motto: "We care for your dog or cat as if they were our own." But the owner's family itself has never had either of these as a pet.

Of course, we'd discussed it. Joey, the oldest, has allergies. So nothing that sheds. Doodle? To designer. Hound? High maintenance. Watchdog or guard? And what's the difference? Melissa always asked.

Over and over, we'd read that book about what kind of dog is right for you, but we'd never settled on one. We'd always been so busy. I've been getting my practice going; we had three children almost in a row and then the whole business of still living in the city —though more on the outskirts, near the water. But, no matter what, someone had to walk the dog. And I knew who that would be.

I muzzled the dog and then examined him. I check his kidneys, teeth, fur, and ears. He wasn't neutered, but there's time for that. It's hard to know if he's had his shots, so I give him the required rabies and distemper. The dog looks at me with deep, soulful eyes as I examine him. If the dog wanted to, he could easily fight me. He could tear me apart. He is a robust and sturdy fellow. But the dog doesn't.

It's near closing, and I put the Closed sign on the door. I gather up some supplies from the office. A choke collar, leash, some bags of treats, and kibble. A squeaky toy and a pig's ear. When I open the door to the kennel, Pirate gets up and stands alert. And when I open the SUV, Pirate jumps right in without hesitating.

I hum to myself on the drive home along the Beltway from my office to home. I smell the ocean breezes while Pirate has his nose sticking out the window, his ears flapping in the wind. This is going to be a great surprise. The best ever. It was better than when I sprang that Presidents' Week trip to Disney World on them (though it had rained the whole time). I can't wait to see their faces, I think, as I pull into the driveway and almost run over Danny's new bicycle that he'd gotten for his birthday.

Oh, those kids. They were always leaving their bikes in the driveway, not to mention their bats and balls and costumes and swords and all the Giants of Justice and Crusader Batman and Dark Knight and Ninja and Avenger action figures. They couldn't pass a store and not beg for some new murderous plastic toy, the names of which I can't keep straight—toys that they just had to have, that were now flung upon the lawn and asphalt, under the trees and in the bushes.

Still smiling, I shake my head. Melissa, I say softly under my breath. I wonder what she does all day long. She isn't much of a cook, and she barely keeps house. "Just raising our family," she'll quip. And they are great kids. Still, thank God Melissa didn't home school them as she'd once contemplated doing. I wonder if they'd even know how to read by this time.

Besides education, the children need discipline, and Melissa isn't very good at that. "Raised by wolves" is what I say when friends come over. Melissa does let them run a little wild. But they are happy kids. That's the main thing, isn't it? So what if some toys get left out? And forgotten.

But those bikes. That does concern me. They shouldn't be riding in the driveway. My father would have had a fit about that. What if a delivery truck pulls in and doesn't see them? Melissa teases me, "Oh, Roger, you worry too much. I mean, what if an asteroid fell on our heads."

She's right. But I worry about the children all the time. I envision worst-case scenarios where Melissa doesn't give them a thought. So I'll try not to worry. I'll bring it up later. Over a glass of wine. Not now. I pull around the bike, put the car in park, and pat Pirate on the head. "Let's go, boy."

In the backyard, Joey is the Prince of Darkness, who, with his rubber sword and mask, is doing battle with Danny. Danny is probably supposed to be invisible in his cape and shield, though Joey, two years older and has infrared sight, can see him. "Take this, you monster." Joey jabs at the air as Danny retreats. Meanwhile, Samantha is rocking on the swing, in conversation with the fairy that sits on her shoulder.

"Hey, guys," I shout, "I've got something for you."

They turn, the three of them, in unison. It's like a moment out of a movie. For an instant, nobody moves. They are frozen in time. I wish that I had a camera ready for this moment. If only they could always be like this. Just as they are at this very instant, their faces are filled with wonder and surprise. I want to shout, "Stop. Nobody move. Stay right where you are." But it's already too late.

They rush toward him, the boys dropping their swords and shields, Samantha forgetting about her fairy, all at once, shouting, "Daddy, Daddy, you brought a dog." They are screaming and jumping up and down, and I worry that the dog might spook because, after all, he'd just been dumped that morning. And who knows what he's been through? But they are all around Pirate, patting him on the head, and Samantha even throws her arms around him, and the dog stands still as if he's always had children hanging from his neck. And then Melissa comes outside, wiping her hands on her jeans, looking at me with a fake scolding finger raised, "I'm not walking him." But there is a twinkle in her eye.

"His name is Pirate," I say.

△△△

We live in the bedroom community of Dunehill, just a few blocks from the sound. We love living there. From the minute we moved in, it became home. We wake to the sea breezes. We live as much outside as we do inside. I run along the beach before seven every other day, and Melissa cycles in the afternoon while the children are at school. They play out there all summer, with adult supervision, of course. Still, there's always been a sense that something was missing. It was like a puzzle, and there was just this one piece, and now we'd found it. What had been missing all along, I realize, as soon as I saw them playing with Pirate, was a dog.

Now the kids are rushing to make Pirate a bed out of some old blankets, and Melissa improvises two Tupperware bowls for water and the Taste of the Wild sample packages of kibble I brought home to see which one Pirate prefers. When I put the bowl on the floor, Pirate sits, not moving, saliva dripping from his mouth. I look at Pirate, and the dog looks at me. It appears that he will not eat without a command. "Okay," I say, pointing to the bowl. The dog rises and eats. "Boy," I say to Melissa, shaking my head. "I wish I could get our children to do that."

Samantha ties a bandanna around Pirate's neck, and they all take turns putting on a leash and walking him around the yard. When Samantha tugs, Pirate doesn't seem to mind. When it is Joey's turn, his eyes don't turn red, and his nose doesn't stuff up. No allergies. That is a good sign. At dinner, I'm afraid that Pirate will beg and give the children strict orders about not feeding the dog under the table, but my fears are groundless. Pirate lies in the corner on his pile of blankets, with one eye on the family, the one surrounded by the black patch, but not once does he come to the table.

When dinner is over, the dog goes to the back door, whimpering, and Melissa and I eye one another in surprise. Melissa smiles, clearly impressed, and I can't hide how pleased I am. "He's not using our backyard as his toilet," Melissa says.

"Of course not," I reply, putting the leash on him and taking him out with Samantha, as I'd promised, to "do his business." After Pirate pisses a river and takes a dump on the sidewalk, which I dutifully clean up using a blue plastic New York Times home-delivery bag, we bring him back inside, where Samantha reports the success of the outing in great detail to her mother. "Well," Melissa says, "he's obviously trained."

That night I take a plastic bucket and put it in the back entryway among the clutter of the winter coats, boots, flip-flops, tennis rackets, and balls strewn everywhere, the scarves and gloves that are stuffed under the bench. How hard is it, I mutter, to clean some of this up? Vowing to move the winter clothes into the basement, I drop Pirate's choke collar and leash and his treats into the bucket. This is where we'll keep his things.

Next, I set up a crate for the dog in the kitchen, but Pirate whines. I move the crate upstairs, between the children's rooms, and throw some treats, but still Pirate whines. "Maybe he doesn't want to be in the crate," Joey, the oldest, says. We let Pirate out. For a few moments, the dog paces between their rooms. Then he finds a place on the floor equal distance between their rooms, circles four times, curls up, and goes to sleep.

When I get up to go for my run in the morning, the dog is waiting for me. He stands outside the bedroom door, which Melissa and I leave open if one of the children needs us in the night, but he hasn't ventured in. He follows me as I walk by in his shorts and running shoes, heading to the front door. Pirate races to the door, wagging his tail. It seems as if the dog wants to run too. I contemplate putting a leash on him, then decide against it. "Okay, boy," I say, patting Pirate on the head. "Let's go."

It is a cool spring morning as we head the few blocks to the beach. A strong breeze blows across the water. At first, I'm concerned that Pirate will run off, but he doesn't. He dashes ahead through the surf and then races back. Once or twice he jumps up onto me with wet paws, but mostly the dog stays at my side. It is incredible to see, really, how Pirate paces me the whole way on my five-mile run.

Even when I was small, I preferred animals to people. That is, I did better with animals. I understood them more—their moods and expressions. I could read an animal in a way that I couldn't read a human. I didn't know when someone was pleased with me or making fun. When someone was giving me the silent treatment, as my mother called it, or just being quiet. I could read the sharper emotions—laughter, a hug, a slap in the face. But the subtler ones —displeasure, impatience, scorn—left me bewildered, and often, I found, I responded in the wrong way. This is why, when I decided to become a doctor, I'd chosen veterinary medicine.

When I leave for work, I put Pirate in his crate. And the dog lies down and goes to sleep. "I guess you wore him out," Melissa says. She offers to take him with her when she goes for her bike ride before everyone gets home from school. In the late afternoon, she calls to tell me, "He ran right along with me the whole way. And when I called him, he came. What were those people thinking when they dropped him off?"

As Melissa puts the kids to bed, I take Pirate for the last walk. Since it is night, I opt to put a leash on him. But as I lead the dog in the darkness, Pirate gets skittish. Shadows and flickers of light make his ears perk. A car honking makes him scramble. I don't notice the hackles going up when the black man appears, carrying a large box. I don't even see the man until Pirate lunges, teeth bared and growling. "Pirate, no." I try to rein him in. The leash tears a strip of skin off my finger.

"I'm sorry," I mumble as the man with the box shakes his head and disappears into his car. Then Pirate turns on me, not biting, but snarling, but rising up on his hind legs. He has a look in his eye, a fiery rage that startles me, and for an instant, I am paralyzed with fear that the dog will attack me. But he doesn't. Pirate stops and settles down, and it is as if the entire episode, whatever it was, had never happened.

Melissa is curled up, watching her favorite show when I get back. She's laughing, the remote in her hand. I think I should tell her, but why make her worry? The dog was startled. Probably all he could see in the darkness were shadows. A little while later, when she comes to bed, I look up at her smiling. I kiss her on the forehead, and we drift to sleep. In the doorway, Pirate's eyes glisten. "It is good, isn't it," Melissa says to me, "to have a dog."

And I whisper back, "It is."

In the morning, I announce that I'll bring Pirate with me to work. Melissa has enough to handle, and besides, the dog follows me everywhere. If I get up in the night to go to the bathroom, the dog waits at the door as I flush. At the office, Pirate lies in a corner on a doggy bed, his eyes open, watching me. He never moves unless I do. My patients' owners comment on it. They call him a sweet dog. They pat him on the head. "He's your dog," one of them says.

△△△

Saturday is one of those first spring days when it's warm enough to spend the whole day outside, so we decide to cycle to Toledo Beach for a picnic. I've wanted to take them on an outing for weeks, but they'd been so busy with school and work. Now Melissa is in the kitchen, cutting the crusts off egg salad and peanut butter sandwiches, and the kids are getting their balls and Frisbees together. And I am pumping air into their bicycle tires.

As I pump, I think about the day ahead. The four of us pedaling along, with Samantha in a child's seat on the back of my bike and Pirate running alongside. It's only a couple of miles in a bicycle lane; nothing the dog hasn't done before. I calculate how far the dog would have to run when I hear the shouting. Shrieking, really, not the kind that comes with a little roughhousing. I dash to the backyard, where I find Danny sobbing and Melissa already on her knees, trying to comfort him. "It's all right," Melissa coos. "Show me."

"What happened?" I say as I clasp Danny in my arms.

Tears stream down his soiled face. "He bit me." Danny points to the dog. Then he bursts into a fresh set of tears. It seemed that Danny had a ball that Pirate wanted, and when Danny tried to snatch it away, the dog had nipped him on the hand.

"Let's see," I say. Danny shows me his wrist. It isn't a bite at all. There is just the slightest red mark. It was nothing. Clearly, the dog has a soft mouth. A dog can tear someone apart if he wants to. I have seen cases. I've put some vicious dogs down, and Pirate isn't one of them. "He didn't mean to hurt you. He thought it was a game. Some dogs are toy possessive. We'll teach him not to be."

But Danny won't stop crying. Each time Pirate approaches, he hides, trembling, behind his mother. It annoys me that Danny is making such a fuss. He's always had that middle-child thing of wanting attention. Everything gets blown out of proportion, and already I sense Melissa wondering if this dog thing is a good idea.

It is a good idea. A family needs a pet. And besides, Pirate is "his dog," people say. I never had a dog that was mine before. The only dog my family ever had was Trickster—a boxer who once pulled my younger brother away from a fireplace fire when a log rolled out. But Trickster attacked the neighbor's dog across the street. A cocker spaniel that had bitten both my brother and me. Trickster got out one afternoon and just went for that dog. I could still hear the sound of the dogs fighting. It wasn't like anything I'd ever heard.

"So, are we going on this outing or not?" I ask, and they agree, though only if Pirate stays home. "That's ridiculous," I say. I'd envisioned a day of tossing balls and Frisbees, Pirate leaping into the air to catch them. All of us bounding into the surf.

"He shouldn't be rewarded," Melissa says. The children are adamant too. So Pirate is left behind. Tail between his legs, he slinks into his kennel without looking at me. Before we go, I slip the dog the pig ear, which he ignores. As we ride away, I hear his howls. We pedal out to Toledo Beach. The sea is a steely gray, and clouds are rolling in. It is colder than we'd anticipated. We eat our sandwiches, toss a ball around, then pedal home.

△△△

On my way to work on Monday, with Pirate riding shotgun, I remember how my father had been so broken up when he'd had to take Trickster to be put down—though, at the time, he'd lied to us, claiming that he was taking him to a farm. It was the only time I'd seen my father look like what could pass for sad. It wasn't until years later, when I was on my way to veterinary school, that I got up the nerve to ask and was told the truth. "Yes," my father told me, his breath sour with the whiskey that would consume his final years, "I put him down."

At the office, I examine Pirate's eyes. They dilate. They aren't milky, and they follow the light. Perhaps certain images just dart past his eyes—the black man with a box in the darkness. Maybe the dog only saw a strange shape. But that wouldn't explain the nipping at the children, would it?

I run the problem by Pete. Not that it is a big problem or anything. Just a matter of concern. Almost in passing, I mentioned that Pirate nipped at Danny but that Danny had been reaching for one of the dog's toys. I don't say the black man with the box at night. Pete, who considers himself a bit of a dog whisperer, has a solution for bad behavior. "Fill a plastic bottle with pennies. Shake it whenever the dog does something you don't like."

△△△

That evening as I pull into my driveway, contemplating putting pennies in a bottle, I almost run over Samantha's tricycle. And Joey's bike is there too, along with the usual assortment of action figures, space weapons, masks, a Batman cape, marbles, plastic ponies, two Ninja swords, and a toy Colt 45 with a pearly white handle, still in its holster. I screech to a halt.

"God, how many times do I have to tell them?" I grumble as I get out and move the bikes to the garage. In passing, I kick some of the toys out of the way, leaving others, which I'll have the children pick up later.

As Pirate races to the back gate, where he barks until Joey opens it for him, I take one blue marble in my hand and roll it down the asphalt and watch as it traverses the sidewalk and slides into the street. That could easily be one of the children, I think, formulating what I will say later to the kids. I shake my head, upset that I need to have this discussion. It isn't just the inconvenience of moving the bikes that bothers me, but the danger. Someone could swing into the driveway and not see one of the children pedaling around. God forbid. I shudder thinking of such a thing. No, it is inconceivable.

Damn it, I mutter under my breath. I wish Melissa would be more responsible. She'd given up her magazine job when we had Joey. She wanted to raise her own kids. But sometimes, it feels as if I have four children instead of three.

I go in and find her in the kitchen, watching a talk show and doing the crossword puzzle. On the stove, a pot of red sauce boils. I come up behind her, smell her scent, and plant a kiss on the back of her neck. I love her neck with its long white curve, over which her dark hair flows, like a swan. I lean in again, and she smells of soap, lavender, I think. I kiss her again, nuzzling against her, but she pulls away, pointing toward the window.

The three kids are in the yard, laughing, shrieking, tossing a ball, and Pirate is yelping, racing back and forth between them. "Pirate, No!" Samantha says, turning in circles as the dog leaps up, trying to capture the ball. Even Danny, who'd been so frightened on Saturday, giggles as he races across the yard. "The children can see us," Melissa says.

Stepping back, I look around at the disarray. Dishes in the sink, toys scattered, clothes scattered. What does she do all day long?

"Busy afternoon, huh?" I said.

"It was my turn to carpool," she replies. "I was just relaxing before I prepared dinner for my master." She answers with the slightest hint of sarcasm. She can be so defensive. But even on days when the housekeeper comes, the place is never in order. It hasn't really bothered me that much before, but now it does.

Over a dinner of spaghetti and green beans, Joey is chattering on about somebody named Arthur who'd said something mean to a girl called Julie, and Danny weighs in that Julie is stupid. I don't even bother pretending to pay attention. I can't get those bikes in the driveway out of my mind. It was careless. They shouldn't even be playing by themselves in the front. Anything could happen.

"What is it?" Melissa reaches across the table, touching my arm. "What's wrong, hon?"

I put down my fork. "I wish I didn't have to keep asking you . . ."

Melissa recoils. "Asking me what?"

"To keep the bikes out of the driveway. To pay attention to what goes on around here." I speak louder than I want to or need to. I try never to raise my voice. I work to keep it in check. I promised myself that I'd never be the way my father was. Constantly losing his temper over nothing, really. The smallest of things, like a light switch left on or if you spilled your juice. Much smaller than this. "You're home all day. Can't you teach them anything?" The children sit back. Pirate's ears perk.

"Roger," Melissa pulls her hand away, "what's come over you?"

Picking up my fork, I shake my head. "Nothing. I'm just tired." Then turning to the children, "Finish your dinner," I say.

△△△

I was hoping for a quiet weekend, just the family, maybe kicking back and watching a ballgame or two, but Melissa has invited a few neighbors and their families. I'd forgotten all about it until she reminded me to buy the briquettes.

"Remember? Barbecue?" She taps my nose with her index finger. I groan, but Melissa reassures me. "It is nothing fancy. Burgers and dogs. Bunch of kids, some backyard softball. It is slated for noon. "A come-and-go," as they call it here in Dunehill. And it's too late to cancel.

By the time I get back from the hardware store, the Jefferys are already here with their twins and the Logans, who live a town away. Cocktails are being served, with Bob Jeffery making appletinis. As the grown-ups sip their drinks, the kids trudge back and forth to the beach, buckets and shovels in hand. Then they settle into a game of softball.

It is getting late, and things are winding down when Joey hits a great line drive. My fist pumps into the air, "Way to go, son!" When he is rounding the bases at full speed, he must have woken Pirate, who was sleeping under a tree, because, in a split second, the dog goes for Joey's ankle.

I see the dog lunge. It is just a split second. Then I hear the sharp cry as my eldest child, crouched on the ground, holds his ankle. "He attacked me," Joey shouts, a tearful wail rising from his throat, disbelief in his eyes. I run over and quickly look at the ankle. On the heel, there are bite marks. Not that hard, not breaking the skin, but bite marks all the same.

"Bad dog," I shout, pointing sharply at the dog. Pirate peers at me in a corner by the side of the house, skulking, tail tucked between his legs. His body trembles as if he is cold.

"Look at him," I say to Joey. "He didn't mean to. You must have startled him. See," I gesture toward the dog, and the dog crawls toward me, though the children cower. "Look how bad he feels."

The barbecue ends shortly after that, with the Logans packing up their salad bowl and the Jefferys with their kids walking back across the street. I keep saying, "Stay, stay. There are more martinis where those came from," but a pall has fallen upon the afternoon as surely as if dark clouds had rolled in. "Our house next time, buddy," Bill Logan says, slapping me on the shoulder as they leave.

As Melissa sits reading that night in bed, I slip into bed, yawning, ready to go to sleep. But Melissa puts her book down. "We need to talk." She turns to me. "I think there might be something wrong with that dog."

"There's nothing wrong with him." I chide her. "I know animals, don't I?"

"Roger, he's gone for two of our children . . . What if it had been one of our guests?" As she shakes her head, her eyes well up.

"He could have hurt them if he'd really wanted to." Even as I say this, I know it isn't much consolation. Still, though Pirate has his issues, I'm sure I can work with him. I look at her sitting there, propped up in her nighty, hair pinned back. Perhaps it is the light in the room, but the lines on her face wrinkle into a grimace that makes her appear for the first time a bit old.

"Do you think I'd bring a dangerous creature into our house?" I say.

Melissa stares up at me with those deep hazel eyes that at times seem to be taunting, judging me. "Not intentionally, no, of course not. But what if he is?"

This is just like her. That "I told you so" side of her. It is as if she's wanted this to fail from the start. She's always been this way, hasn't she? But I've ignored it until now. She has to have the last laugh, the upper hand. She has that smug way of someone who always needs to be correct. "Okay," I flare up. "If that's what you want . . ."

I get up and walk away. Her hand goes to her mouth. "Roger, this isn't like you . . ." Before she can finish, I slam the bedroom door. That night I fell asleep in the den, watching old horror films. It will be dawn before I come back to the bedroom.

At the breakfast table, I explained to the children that I would look for a new home for Pirate. One where he has more room to be free. "I'll find him a big farm where he can run and play."

Tears start to slip down Samantha's face, and Danny's eyes well up too. Pirate stares from his place in the corner. His ears perk up when he hears his name.

"He's not that bad, Dad," Danny says. "It's just sometimes he can be a little scary . . ." Even Joey, who'd made such a fuss when the dog nipped him, is nodding.

I look over at Melissa, whom I can see is caving in. "You're right," she shrugs. "It's just sometimes." Because I believe that a family is a democracy, we have a vote. It is unanimous.

"We'll get a trainer," I say. "That'll solve things."

△△△

That night as I take Pirate out for his usual walk, Ted Baxter, a neighbor, stops to chat. Ted has some bags in his hands and a briefcase, coming home late with Chinese food that he'll eat over a hockey game, "if the wife will let me," and, as he puts the bags down to shift them, Pirate growls, rises on his hind legs and lunges, tugging hard at the leash. I try holding him back, almost slicing into my finger again in the process, as Ted grabs his bags and backs away. "I hope you're insured," Ted says as he walks off toward his house.

As I try to rein in the dog, Pirate turns on me. White teeth flashing, eyes almost on fire, the dog growls from some deep guttural place and snaps at my hand. I'm shaking, my heart racing, not only because I fear the dog but because it seems so familiar. It is a look I'd seen before, but I can't remember exactly when or where. Then the rage leaves as quickly as it came. "Sit," I say, and Pirate sits at my side.

Melissa is reading in bed, the light of her Kindle illuminating her face. "It took you a while to get home. Anything wrong?"

She's waiting for me to hear about what happened as if she senses it was important. I feel it. The way she lies there, staring at me, stretched out in her nighty.

I hesitate. I should tell her. I've always told her everything. But I don't this time. Instead, I shake my head. "Everything's fine." In the corridor, the dog spins in circles outside the children's rooms, lies down, and goes to sleep.

"Roger, something's not right . . ."

What's bothering me most is the dog's unpredictability. Pirate could lunge at a scooter, a jogger, a cardboard box. Or he could just as easily pay it no heed. I never know when the dog will go for something and when he isn't. In my heart, I believe that Pirate isn't a bad dog, just a fearful one, and if I can just penetrate the source of his fear, I will understand the dog.

Of course, I have no idea what life Pirate lived before. Or why the owners dropped him off at his clinic. Now I think about how some creatures are violent because they are evil, while others lash out when afraid.

"Not right with Pirate?" I ask.

"With Pirate, yes, and . . ." Melissa says, gazing down, "with us. You haven't been yourself."

"There's nothing wrong with us," I say, pursing my lips. "You're just on edge. You need to relax." I touch her arm softly, with a romantic edge to it.

"Get some rest," she responds, turns, and puts out her bedside lamp.

I lie awake while my wife sleeps, her back towards me, while in the hallway, Pirate paces. The dog is restless too. I sit up and look toward the door. In the darkness, I can make out Pirate's form. A pair of eyes glisten in the moonlight.

△△△

Carl is a huge Jamaican man with a bad hip and can barely make it up the front steps. He wears a hoodie and carries a huge black plastic bag filled with newspaper. As has been prearranged, when Carl rings the doorbell, Melissa and I step back. Then Carl bursts in like gangbusters, hoodie pulled tight, banging the plastic bag in the air. Pirate growls and lunges at the bag, barking and baring his teeth; then, after a few moments, the dog skulks away.

"You smell that?" Carl says, once he is safely inside and Pirate is on a leash. Carl is sniffing the air, and Melissa and I join him. There is a musty odor. "That's his anal glands. I'm sorry, but that's his fear. He's afraid. Your dog is afraid."

Carl comes highly recommended. "If a dog can be cured," a client told me, "Carl can do it." Carl diagnoses Pirate's problem as "fear aggression." "Very treatable, fixable," Carl mutters in a hard-to-understand West Indian accent. He says something about six sessions in a row—every morning at eight before I go to work—and an electric collar with a remote control that costs "an arm and a leg" but is worth it. "You must give him a little shock," Carl says. "Let him know who's boss."

Then Carl shows how the collar works. "Page" for when you want him to come. "Nick" for when you want him to stop whatever he's doing. And "continuous" for when he is being very bad.

After Carl leaves, I plug the remote and collar into the charger in the entryway. Then I find Melissa, who's sitting in their living room.

"I feel as if I'm torturing him with this electric collar," Melissa says, eyes down as she picks at a piece of lint on the sofa. "Maybe we should find Pirate another home."

Melissa sighs. She's tired of it, I can tell. But we can't give up on this dog. It's as if the dog chose us. As if there's some purpose behind all of this. Something we have yet to understand. "No matter what," I tell Melissa, "we can't give the dog away the way he is. He's got to be trained even if we adopt him out."

"He's bitten two of our children."

"He didn't hurt them. He could have easily . . ."

"It's not just that." Tears rise in her eyes. "It's us as well. We don't go for walks in the morning anymore. And if we do, it's always with Pirate, and you have to keep an eye on him," she tells me. "And we don't lie in bed. You're always getting up with that dog . . ."

I bristle. "He's not that dog. He is our dog."

"It's as if he matters to you more than we do."

I shake my head. "That's not true, Mel. You know it's not true." I reach out my arms. "Come here." But she's already walking away.

△△△

On the beach in the morning, as the surf pounds the shore, Carl puts Pirate on a thirty-foot lead, in a choke collar, with the electric collar as well. "He looks like a gladiator," Melissa quips, and she and I laugh. "Here, Spartacus," she calls.

"Don't confuse him," Carl says.

We walk him up and down the boardwalk. Carl watches as Pirate lunges at a cyclist, a kid on a scooter. "Leave it," Carl says. With each lunge, Carl zaps him.

As the days wear on, Melissa and I watch in amazement as Pirate ignores cyclists and children, bouncing balls. He doesn't glance at big men carrying packages or sanitation workers toting garbage cans. If they just show him the remote, he grows docile. "You see," Carl says, "this dog learns fast. He's not afraid no more. And he knows you're boss."

By the end of the week, there's no more reason to zap Pirate. If the dog so much as sees the remote, he stops dead in his tracks and, tail between his legs, retreats. He drops something when he hears "leave it." He ignores all the things that frightened him before. Melissa has to admit it's like having a new dog.

On Friday, Pirate graduates from Carl's Canine Academy, and that night I slip into bed beside my wife. I reach for her. "Welcome back," she says.

"It's better, isn't it?" I kiss her neck. "Things are better."

"Yes, they are." Cradling my head, she whispers into my ear and kisses me back.

△△△

On Sunday morning, we linger in bed. I make a pot of coffee and bring it to her. When Joey comes in, we tell him to watch cartoons with Danny and Samantha. Joey does a fist pump into the air. "Cartoons, yeah!" As we lie in bed curled up, we can hear the Looney Tunes theme song. I make a Woody Woodpecker imitation in her ear, and Melissa laughs.

I'm pulling her closer, snuggling against her chest, when we hear the screams. We've heard them a million times before. A toy being fought over, some minor power struggle such as one finds among siblings. Probably Joey wants to change the station to watch his Power Rangers program, and the other kids are protesting. But the screams go on. They are different. Not like any we've heard before. And they don't stop.

I scramble, shouting, pulling on my pajama bottom as Melissa sweeps out of bed, into a robe, both dashing as fast as we can down the few stairs and into the living room to find Pirate with his jaws locked around Samantha's skull. In her hands, Samantha clutches the dog's rubber bone. Her mouth is open in a continuous scream as rivulets of blood flow through her blonde curls and down her face.

Pirate holds her perfect head like a ball he intends to play with. The louder she screams, the harder he seems to hold on. Melissa, sobbing, and gasping, tries to pry her daughter away, but the dog growls and holds fast. I shout, slamming the dog with my fists. The dog glares back at me, his eyes on fire, but he doesn't let go. Now I know where I'd seen that look in his eyes before. I've seen it all my life. Nothing puts more fear into me than that look. I clasp the dog's jaws, but the dog does not let go.

Then I remember the remote. Even though Pirate doesn't have the collar on, he's terrified of the remote. I dash into the back entryway, tossing discarded sweatshirts and muddy shoes aside, digging into the plastic bucket that holds the dog's things—treats, collars, but not the remote. I toss down coats, fling boots out of the way until I see it, plugged into the wall where I'd left it charging. Grabbing it, I dash back into the family room, holding the remote up for the dog to see. "Leave it," I shout, pushing the button. Cowering, Pirate lets go of Samantha's head. He puts his tail between his legs and skulks away. And the dog's inexplicable and pointless rage is gone.

As Melissa rushes to her sobbing daughter, I grab the dog and drag him into his kennel. Back in the family room, they are all crying. Danny has wet his pants. Joey trembles behind the sofa. "Look at her." Melissa points, shrieking and sobbing, at their bleeding child, "Look what you've done." Samantha looks up, and I see she's not only afraid of the dog. She's scared of me.

I throw the boys, still in their pajamas, into the backseat. Melissa and Samantha are in front, a towel wrapped around the little girl's head. She's stopped crying now, except for hiccups of sobs, but she stares at me with red, angry eyes. At the hospital, they shave her yellow curls and sew twenty-two stitches across her skull. The bite has narrowly missed her right eye. The scars will probably disappear by the time she grows up.

When we get home, I put a leash on Pirate and drive him to the clinic. Pete, who's at the desk, looks up in surprise. He rises, offering to help, but I shake my head. "I'm doing this alone," I say. I lead Pirate into the room with the cold marble slab—the one I use for such purposes. I put the dog on the table, and Pirate lies right down, face between his paws. The dog looks at me, as always, with his dark eyes. As I approach with the needles, Pirate doesn't turn away.

The first injection is to calm him down. Pirate doesn't budge. He looks so peaceful it's hard to imagine that this dog has a vicious bone in his body. The fury came and went so quickly. Now the dog raises his face and licks my hand. This gesture startles me so much that I almost begin to cry.

I sigh, think back to when my father took my first dog away, and then I plunge the lethal dose into Pirate's neck. It paralyzes the heart, and in moments, my dog is dead.

A FINAL PORTRAIT
OF A DAUGHTER

Our youngest girl, Bernadette —who everyone called Bernie, hasn't looked this pretty in, well, forever. The mortician who worked on her did not ask for a photo; instead he went with his feelings about how she should look. He couldn't have been more wrong, from head to toe.

We remember her as a tomboy, and she was until the end, at age 23, pale and skinny, and never wore make-up. How would she react to her new image now? Big hair, bright red lips, and flawless eyebrows.

Did the mortician really see her in his mind that way? Or is that the way he always prepared young women? Does he have a portrait gallery of them? His subjects all, pale and transcendent with wavy tresses, like a doll.

It wasn't that long ago that our daughter told us she'd found her niche, as an athlete, in a sport that required her to be in shape, to watch her weight, lift weights, and be in the gym for many hours.

And that wasn't all. She also discovered drugs. Who needs calories, she'd say. Our girl had chlorinated laps for breakfast, a climbing wall for lunch, and a treadmill for dinner, gripping handlebars her collar bones now resemble.

Meanwhile, her womanly hipped friends were meeting at the Pizza place and ordering extra cheese, extra sauce, and extra everything, to go along with their sugary drinks. And that was before they had desert —of course.

I suppose we should thank the mortician, because long after the starving is over, we'll have our girl's image, at least, hanging in our living room: her skeletal fingers holding a bouquet, which oddly enough looks like cherries and cream.

POETIC LOVE AND LICENSE

One day, I met Alice in a courthouse and fell for her on the spot. I was an attorney then for a small law firm specializing in slip and fall cases… lots of them, handed to us by runners who found them in hospital waiting rooms for which we paid $50 a case. This, as you might guess, is the law as practiced at the low end of the judicial system. But that was all I expected after graduating from a non-accredited law school, and I was happy enough to work at any law firm.

On the other hand, she had graduated from a top ABA school and looked it. Alice stood in the center of the hallway outside the courtroom, waiting to meet and confer with someone on a case, back straight, bobbed dark hair, black pinstriped suit, pearls. Did the ray of sun that spotlighted her to me come from the heavens? I always thought so.

She looked young and innocent, but by then, she was 32, and she'd earned an undergraduate and a masters degree in public affairs from UC Irvine, taught for a while there, and then attended law school at that same place. Along the way, she'd learned Spanish and French, Italian and Japanese, and picked up a passable Portuguese. She could recite Seventeenth-century French poetry at the drop of a chocolate macaroon that she had baked herself.

I didn't know what a macaroon was before I tasted what seemed like eating a sweet piece of a cloud. What instilled in me the courage to talk to her, let alone think I could date her, is a puzzle to me even now.

Our conversation was a success because Alice made it so. If she were the world-renowned violinist playing Vivaldi, I was the chimpanzee trying to mimic the movements of her bow. A million times since—in the eight years during which we've managed to date, marry, and do a few other things—I've asked myself: Why would a woman like that give a guy like me the time of day?

The answer is simple: Wally.

Wally's the one flaw in Alice's accomplished life, the thing this highly successful woman contended with like a thorn in her shoe. He's Roger Clinton to Bill Clinton, the mad first wife of Maxim de Winter in Rebecca, and Richard III. Or maybe he's the dirt you get under your fingernails from climbing your way to the top, proof you didn't start out there and maybe didn't belong. Regardless, a brother like Wally makes a guy like me look good—husband-material good. Because others left Alice —they ran away from her as fast as they could after meeting Wally.

There are limits, though, and Wally may have reached his earlier this morning with the phone call. I knew it was him because afterward, Alice crossed the kitchen, bathrobe parted a hair too wide. She had that look on her face as if she'd just robbed a jewelry store and knew she'd get away with it.

"It's not happening, Alice."

She placed a hand over my mouth. "He's my brother."

Alice hasn't been back to Wellston in the nine years I've known her. As far as I know, she hasn't seen Wally in that time, either.

"Fine," I said. "But this is huge. We're talking my-whole-weekend-shot-and-you-owe-me-a-new-set-of-clubs huge."

She smiled and silently exited, sashaying her thanks.

"We're talking the nice Epon clubs," I shouted after her. "Driver and all!"

△△△

Wally has two arrests for narcotics possession, a few assault charges that got knocked down to misdemeanors, and community service. One six-month stint in Southeastern Correctional for possession of stolen goods—a Harley Softail he bought off a friend for the red-flag-inducing low price of seventy-eight dollars.

Wally isn't wholly responsible, I'm told. When he was eighteen, there was a fight or some other incident, and his brain got rattled, not enough to make him a vegetable but enough to tear away little chunks of his inhibition. Alice has hinted about the circumstances but never answered my questions. She's suggested, in some way, it was her fault. When I ask her to elaborate, she always deflects.

"I'll explain someday," she says. "Just not now."

△△△

After the seven-hour drive from Irvine to Wellston, Nevada, I pull up to the house Wally rents from an elderly pastor. This is the only place Wally's lived for more than a few months. When Wally works, he works as a substitute mailman. Even with his record, he wangled the gig out of a buddy he knew at the post office. But it's part-time and doesn't draw much cash. Wally's been evicted at least half a dozen times from other places. He's going on four years here, and I suspect it's the pastor's abundant well of forgiveness. That or Wally supplies the old guy with weed.

The house is massive. Two and a half stories with a dome and wraparound porch. It's fallen into disrepair, graying paint on the wooden siding, shingles clipped away by the wind, and one window knocked out and replaced with particleboard. Livable only by squatters' standards.

I climb the stairs and press the doorbell. When I hear nothing, I knock.

"You looking for me?"

I turn around to see Wally standing in the oil-stained yard. He's wearing a purple "Race for the Cure" T-shirt about a size too small. A slight disruption in the hair on the left side of his head hints at the scar that slides up into his scalp. He's sprouted a mustache since I last saw him, and he's wearing dark sunglasses that pinch his nose.

"Yes, Wally," I say. "I'm looking for you." I'm set to deliver my speech, but he charges up the stairs, swings his arm around my shoulders, and whisks me into the house. I can't say whether or not I'm going of my own free will.

Inside is a wide hallway leading all the way to the back. The house used to be a funeral home. The bottom floor contains three large rooms—two to the left and one to the right—each with its own set of sliding double doors. What an awful day it must have been in the small town of Wellston when they needed all three of those rooms at once. Some mining accident, maybe. Three men on the same day. The mourners slipping between services. The heavy doors sliding on their runners like whispers in the wood.

Now, though, the house is dark and quietly stale. I get the impression there hasn't been electricity on in a long time. In the front room is a shabby living space. A Coleman lantern rests on a stool next to a left-leaning recliner, which looks as if it's been hauled out of a dumpster.

Walking toward the back of the house, Wally says, "You didn't tell Alice anything, did you?"

"What do you mean? You talked to Alice."

He presses a finger to his forehead. I smell sweat but no alcohol.

"Are you high?" I say.

He tilts his sunglasses down to show me the state of his eyes. The hallway is so dim his irises are nothing but dark little sockets. A wave of fear ripples through my stomach.

"Wally, what is this?"

He points deeper into the house. "Back here."

He keeps his arm around me. We stride slowly, hip to hip. To my right, the room is closed, but the oak doors have been warped from a leak in the ceiling. They no longer slide together correctly. Through the crack, I see that the floor of the room beyond is covered with stacks of small rectangular piles. Letters.

Thousands upon thousands, by my guess.

"Wally."

"Not there."

"Wally, what the hell?"

He turns to face me and holds my wrists. His breath—definitely not alcohol. Just the lingering smell of a breakfast burrito.

"Look," he says. "I do these mail routes, right? Sometimes I lighten the load. Just trash, okay? Junk mail. People don't want that shit anyway. Saves everybody a hassle."

"Just junk mail," I repeat.

"That's right. But I keep it all. Just in case. If somebody ever says —if they go, 'Wally, I don't get credit card offers anymore,' then maybe I find their stuff and I throw in a couple."

"Has anyone ever said that?"

"No. Mostly, the routes are rural—mailboxes on the road. I drive my car. I don't talk to residents."

"You can still deliver the letters." I'm babbling. "All of it's in there?"

"I'm not worried about that."

"It's a federal offense, Wally." I'm talking in whispers like the place is bugged. "That's prison, Wally. Real prison."

"I already did prison." He says it like it's a one-off thing, similar to mandatory military service.

"You could dole it out over several weeks, get rid of the out-of-date coupons. Burn them." I'm surprised at how quickly I'm considering the angles. Is that how criminals speak?

Wally shakes his head. He slips the sunglasses back over his eyes. In the lenses, I'm a weak reflection of myself.

"That's not why I called," he says. He ushers me back to the last room and slides back the door to reveal a single, very short pile of letters. It sits in the center of a bare floor. It's like an art installation. The blinds are all drawn, and thin slats of light rake the floorboards.

"Sometimes I get lonely," he says. He sits on the floor and holds his hands over the stack like he's warming himself over the embers of a campfire.

"It's where I got my problem," he says.

It's hard to distinguish details, but one thing's clear. Every one of these letters—about two or three dozen—has been opened. They're all stacked, their frayed ends to the right, so they lean to the left like the recliner in the front room.

I'm moaning as I step forward. Words escape me in whimpering, girlish syllables. "What did you do, Wally? God damn it, what did you do?"

"I ain't never asked for help before. You know that. But I'm asking it now."

It's a ridiculous statement. Wally's begged favors a thousand times and squeezed friends and relatives for money his whole life. But none of that matters now. I think of Alice.

"What kind of help do you need?" I say. "If it's something illegal—"

He waves me off. "I need you to drive me somewhere. I need you to help me smooth things over. It's a girl."

"What girl?"

He slaps his knees and rubs his thighs without looking up. He's just staring at the letters.

"Wally, what girl?"

He looks up, and his usual half-grin is gone. All I can see is the smooth whites of his cheeks below his sunglasses.

"I'm in love, Roger. We're in love."

Wally insists I read at least a few of the letters.

"So you understand," he says.

They're from a woman named Maria Rodriguez, and they're addressed to her grandmother, also named Maria. It's the usual stuff, asking about the older woman's welfare, the state of her house, and other members of the far-flung family. What's immediately evident, however, is the woman's gift for language.

While her questions to the elder Maria verge on the mundane, her descriptions of her own life—her updates about days spent in the shade of her backyard, amid friends at church functions, in movie theaters, or on errands—flow like rivers of cool water across murmuring stones.

The younger Maria's letters seem to be a freeing exercise for her creative spirit. In one, she writes, "Gold nasturtiums pucker at the pale moon." In another, on a trip to a local beauty pageant, she describes a scene as "the glistering lips of dolled-up little girls."

And she has a tender devotion to her grandmother, whom she calls "Nana." Maria's care and warmth pour onto every page. She evokes familial longing and the pang of some old loss.

I hand a letter to Wally. "What am I supposed to get out of this?"

"You don't feel it? It's poetry, man. She's genuine."

The thought of Wally swooning over infinite beauty disturbs me. Wally is all base desire, drug addictions, cons, a broken parade of chain-smoking lovers, and back-alley affiliations.

"So what if it's poetry?" I say. "You stole this woman's letters. What the hell were you thinking?"

"I was thinking; I'm in love."

"That is not—what? Why would you even say that?"

"It's not like I do it to everybody, man. It's not like I'm opening all the mail of everybody on my route. That'd be ridiculous. I saw her, okay. She's beautiful. You can't believe how beautiful. And then with the letters, you know, she's beautiful on the inside too."

"Whatever it is, Wally, whatever you've done—you need to work it out."

"You have to help me," he says. "You have to vouch for me."

"Why would I do that?"

"We started writing to each other."

That moan escapes me again.

"Is it her husband, Wally? Is that it? Or is it a jealous boyfriend? Did you rile this guy, smash out his windows?"

"Nothing like that."

"Wally, are we talking police involvement? Just tell me."

"It's her dad," he says. "I need you to talk to her dad."

And right there, it hits me. I hold out my arm like a crossing guard.

"Yeah," he says. "You caught me. She's fifteen."

△△△

Alice finally answers the fourth time I call.

"What is it, Roger? I'm working."

"Did he tell you what this was about?"

"He didn't. He doesn't tell me anything."

"This is criminal, Alice."

"He's my brother."

"I don't care if he's your brother. He says he's in love with a fifteen-year-old girl. They're pen pals."

She hesitates. Finally, she mutters, "Oh, Jesus."

"Is this about something in his past?" I say. "Is Wally some kind of —" I lower my voice "—you know, pedophile?"

"Stop it," she says.

"Tell me otherwise, Alice. Say it straight out."

"I'm sure it's not that," she says.

"He stole her mail. There's a little old lady out there wondering why her granddaughter never writes. That's federal, Alice."

"He has problems. It's nothing as bad as you say. I just need you to do this for me, Roger. He can't take another strike. You know that better than anybody."

"This goes way beyond golf clubs."

"Do whatever he needs you to do."

"Simple as that, huh?"

"Simple as that. Do it for me," she says. "It's important. Last time I'll ask."

"You're too good," I say. "You're like an angel."

"I'm not," she says and hangs up.

△△△

We're driving up a two-lane road into a patch of backwoods where the sunlight's gone gray. The hills churn up further and further into more and more remote tangles of trees until we're passing an old logging lane and turning off onto a gravel side road.

Wally sits beside me, tapping his thigh. He's still wearing the sunglasses despite the deep shade from the trees.

"I love her, man," he says. "You understand that, right? You got Alice, man. You love Alice. So you understand." He turns toward me. His arm is propped on the dash, leaning against the door.

The oddest feeling comes over me. He's not wearing his seat belt, and I think I might be able to shoot my arm past him, pull the handle, and kick him into the ditch.

I shake my head to clear that thought. "Alice," I say, "has the good sense to stay away from you. Alice—I don't want you bringing her into it."

"Of course, I'm bringing Alice into it. You guys have something special. You should know special when you see it. If anybody should understand, it's you."

He lights a cigarette, and I don't stop him. I'm picking my battles.

"And Alice," he says, "for your information, stays away because she knows what she did."

"What do you mean, 'what she did,' Wally?"

"Nothing, man."

"Alice," I say, "isn't fifteen. Alice and I were adults when we met. We're adults now. You're an adult now."

"Don't matter. You woulda known, man. That's my point. If you'd met Alice when she was fifteen and you were eighty, it wouldn't matter. You'd know. Soul mates forever."

For all his idiocy, Wally assumes Alice and I are cosmically bonded. And Alice, on her part, has never given me a reason to doubt it. But I've always thought I lucked into Alice loving me. I'm always waiting for her to wake up one day and come to her senses—hop out of bed, pack her bags, leave me, and never return.

"God damn it, Wally. You swear to God you haven't done anything with this girl? Nothing illegal?"

"Except the mail stuff?"

"The letters, yes. Other than stealing her mail. You promise you haven't—"

"Dinged her?"

"Had sex, anything like that? Anything remotely like that?"

"I promise. I'd wait forever for this girl."

I slow the car as the road turns into an endless series of washed-out ruts. "I absolutely cannot believe I'm a part of this right now."

"You're family now, man, kinfolk. I'd do the same for you." He points. "It's up there."

A gravel drive leads up a hill to a rustic cabin to the right. I stop the car at the bottom of the drive. The lawn area is all overgrown up and reverted to its natural state. It looks like that scene at the beginning of Little House on the Prairie. I half expect Maria Rodriguez to come bounding down in a bonnet.

"What now?" I say.

"I just need you to be like a character witness."

"You've talked to this man?"

"Maria talked to him. He's home tonight."

△△△

It's almost dark when we reach the entrance of the house. There's a cast-iron knocker on the door in the shape of a fist. I'm trying to draw conclusions about this man I'm supposed to—what am I supposed to tell this guy? What can a guy with a fifteen-year-old daughter think when another man, twenty years older than his daughter, shows up with another guy to help "explain the situation," as Wally puts it? What can the father be thinking? I know what I'd be thinking, and its articulation might involve a firearm.

Wally pulls the knocker and drops it, making a loud clunk on the door. The door opens immediately.

The guy has to be seven feet tall. The top of the doorway hides his forehead. I take a step back. He looks Latino with wide, high cheekbones and a jaw that juts forward like a brick. He's as wide as Wally and I put together. Behind him, what little I can see of the room looks cozy, bright with a low fire in the fireplace. Books line the thick oak shelves built into the wall. There's a dark leather chair in the corner.

"I've been expecting you," he says.

Wally nods like he has won the first round—yes, yes, we're here to talk business. The man steps aside, and we walk in.

"I'm Wally," Wally says.

"Tomás," says the man.

I mumble my name—"Roger"—as I slide past him.

"Wally, Tomás, and Roger," says Wally, slapping his thigh as if what he said was poetic.

"Is that supposed to be funny?" Tomás says. His frown indicates the opposite.

He leads us back through a new granite-tiled kitchen with a massive island and a cooking range. There's no sign of the girl. We walk out onto the back patio, where a fire pit has been cut out of the middle of the decking. He motions for us to sit. Wally continues standing, and I stand with him.

A few steaks are sizzling on a low-lying grill over a cast-iron pot of burning applewood. Tomás flips the steaks, and for the first time, after getting past his size, I notice he's wearing a neat white apron. Wally and I must have interrupted the grilling process. I hope we aren't responsible for ruining his steaks on top of everything else.

"Where's Maria?" Wally says.

Tomás doesn't stop, but there's a ripple in the enormous muscles of that broad back. It's a split-second quiver like a horse flinching under an insect bite. "She won't be joining us," he says.

"Where is she?"

"I wanted us to talk this out, like men." He fusses over the steaks with a pair of tongs.

"I don't know about that, man," Wally says.

That whole back muscle thing again, only more so now.

"Come on, Wally," I say in a whisper. "Let's not start on a bad note."

Wally takes the hint when I grip his forearm. I motion for him to sit down in one of the Adirondack chairs.

"Pour yourself a drink," Tomás says.

I notice three tumblers on the table, and, at Wally's request and with Tomás's consent, I pour us all three fingers of Johnnie Walker Black Label.

"Too bad you ain't got the Blue Label," Wally says. "I ain't never tried that." He puts his feet up on a little wooden ottoman. His biker boots jingle as the chains around his ankles settle.

"I have the Blue Label," Tomás says without adding more.

"Maria says you were some kind of football star."

Again the flinch. Tomás draws in his huge right arm almost involuntarily.

"I played for the Oilers," he says.

"Is that still a team?"

"No."

"Austin?"

"Houston," Tomás says.

"Warren Moon," I say, trying to placate.

"I played offensive tackle," Tomás says. "I protected Warren for seven years. I'm a man used to protecting."

For want of something to add, I say, "That's interesting."

Tomás doles out the steaks and puts them on sturdy green plates, rustically thick and textured. There's nothing else. Nothing but the steak and the whiskey. He hands us each two knives, no forks. We sit around the fire, cutting and eating like cavemen.

Wally and Tomás stare at each other. I wait for the conversation to begin, but it doesn't. The steak is thick, and the only sounds are chewing and swallowing. After a while, the silence gets to me. I finally say, "What can we do to make this right?"

Tomás looked at me as if I had just arrived and was butting into a private conversation. A wad of steak is in his mouth. He finishes it off slowly and swallows.

"You can leave my daughter alone," he says. "You can do that, and I won't press charges. And if you ever contact her again, I promise to kill you."

I'm trying to be calm, to ignore the threat. I turn to Wally. "He's right. You have to stop seeing her. That's fair, Wally."

Wally sets down the two knives and picks up the steak with his fingers. He takes a bite of the steak the way a hyena tears into a zebra's haunch. A trickle of blood rolls down the side of his hand. He chews twice and swallows hard because the piece is way too big.

Wally turns toward me and says, "I tell you what, Roger, how about you tell this big son-of-a-bitch I'll wait till she's eighteen, or he comes around and signs the papers to get married when she's sixteen. I ain't giving up. Not on love. She's a poet, and she's touched my soul."

"I think he can hear you, Wally."

Still ignoring Tomás, he says, "I'm not giving her up. Not even if it means I got to fight to the death."

Wally lets the steak drop from his hand to the patio. It makes a fleshy smack on the treated wood. He sets down his plate and scoops up the steak knives.

Everything slows down. There's a fire dying in the house. There's a fire dying here in front of us. The sun is tilting away into the hill. The low stir of our breathing is alive with possibility.

"Don't let this get out of hand, Wally."

"You read the letters, Roger."

"They aren't worth dying over."

"Love is always worth dying over."

Tomás is a mountain in the dusk.

"You're talking stupid," I say.

"Am I?"

There's a fevered look in his eye.

△△△

About ten years after that evening, when our daughter, Claire, is all but grown-up, Alice and I will be home alone, and for some reason, Alice will look wistful and jumpy. She'll be biting her nails and standing, then sitting and standing again. I'll beg her to tell me what's on her mind.

"Wally," she'll say. "Claire being out tonight makes me think of Wally. Things changed between us when we were teenagers," she'll say. "I was in high school, and we'd always been close, but things changed."

Alice's story will be about a girl. Herself thirty years earlier. Sixteen, with dark brown hair cut short, her acid-washed jeans tight, showing off all she's got, which is a lot. The girl has on a yellow T-shirt with a screen-print logo—a local pizza joint. It's hot for this late in September, and the band is still playing over the hill in a post-football-game salute that rises out of the high school stadium along with the white lights blotting out a portion of the stars.

She's walking the tracks because it's a shorter way home to a trailer park near the fire station. Everyone was at the game, and they're all just now leaving it with whoops and whistles. The Rockets won, and the cars not far off, on the main drag, are separated from this girl by a spindly barrier of trees, a muddy brook full of Mountain Dew cans and cigarette butts, and old milk cartons. Nearby are a couple of rust-mottled sheds tagged with graffiti. A blotchy blue scrawl announces that Eddie loves Wanda like crazy.

The tracks are quiet.

Three young men are only fifty yards away. They haven't seen her yet, but they will. About two miles back, as they walked into town, they passed a rickety farm, and two of the boys killed a couple of baby rabbits in their hutch just to see what it felt like. They broke the rabbits' necks by twisting their heads. The third boy didn't participate, but he watched and didn't say anything. He smoked a cigarette and put it out under his boot near the place where one of the boys threw a rabbit down. The third boy walked away after that, and it's the only thing that kept the other two from killing the remaining rabbits where they slept.

The two killers are red-faced, bleach-eyed, and freckled from three weeks under the sun, working on framing up a barn. They've been paid under the table each Friday, and on the third Friday—tonight —they left for good with dreams of sex and a little pot, if they can get it. They heard there's a party in a field outside town after the game, and there'll be girls there, high school kids only a little younger than themselves.

They see the girl when she sees them, and one boy chuckles. He's killed a rabbit, and he's chuckling about the girl on the train tracks with her arms crossed under her breasts prominent in a thin yellow T-shirt.

He thinks of convincing her to fool around with him in the woods. He asks if she likes beer.

She says she's headed home.

The boy who did not kill a rabbit stands back in the dark, not moving forward like the other two, not talking.

When the girl tries to push past, the two rabbit killers throw her to the ground. There's a sound of tearing cotton and the screech of the rail bed shifting under boots and hands. That's when something snaps in the mind of the third boy, and he says, "Stop!"

They ignore him. He's seething now, looks around, and picks up a rock from the creek bed. It's a jagged stone, the weight of a book. He steps behind the other two boys who have pinned the girl to the ground. He raises the stone and slams it into them: the first one on his back and the second on his shoulder. A deep gash on the first boy makes the blood run out a hole in his shirt.

The boy with the stone gets in a few more blows before one of the other two swings something at him and strikes him in the head.

He shudders but keeps pounding them with the rock until they flee.

Now the boy is standing alone with the rock still in his hand. He stares at the girl with her shirt torn down to her navel, her bra torn. She's indecent because she isn't thinking of covering herself. She's trying to refasten the button on her jeans, but it's not there. The button has flown off into the woods, and the boy thinks he might come back and look for it later in the daylight in case she can sew it back on.

For now, though, the girl is indecent in the spill of stadium light working through the trees. He sees her breasts. Then her face. Recognition. Her breasts are whiter than he remembers from years ago when she was still unashamed to show him her body. It's hard for him to think of her as his sister right now.

"I'm sorry," he says. "I didn't know it was you. I—I love you," he says, and he has no idea what he means by it.

In the scuffle, one of the other boys has struck him with something, maybe a piece of iron from the rail bed. Whatever it was, it made an extended cut in his skull above his ear. He's shivering now, looking at the girl. The sight of her is exciting and familiar. His hand shakes so bad he drops the rock.

"I love you," he says again. Again he has no idea what he means by it.

Sitting in our living room, Alice will say, "Wally was never very bright before then. But that incident made it worse. And his brain just got stuck at that point. It was like he never gave up trying to undo what happened that night, trying to make it right."

"I failed Wally," Alice says, "because I didn't know how to take care of him after that. His mind wasn't right. He needed my help, but I've never been able to provide it. And how could I? I couldn't change the past."

ΔΔΔ

Wally lurches forward with a steak knife gripped in either hand. The blades are pointed down, and he raises his arms over his head. He leaps past the fire pit at Tomás, and I have to believe, to this day, that his intention was only to scare Tomás, not to stab him.

The speed and strength with which Tomás reacts is impressive. He tucks in his right arm and punches Wally between the sternum and windpipe, just over Wally's heart. There's a cracking sound. The knives fly from Wally's hands. Wally cartwheels over the deck chair, landing like a tossed doll.

Tomás rises to his feet.

I step in front of him.

"Don't do it," I say. "He's down."

For a moment, I think he's going to hit me. He's thinking about it.

"I don't think he meant that. He was just overreacting, which he sometimes does," I say.

"I should call the police."

"We don't need the police to take care of this. Wally's thing with your daughter will blow over," I say. "Just give it time. Wally may seem older age-wise, but he's really mentally and socially immature as a fifteen-year-old, maybe even younger."

Tomás looks back at Wally, who's unconscious, and nods slightly.

"As I said before, I want to take care of things."

"How do you want to do that?" Tomás says.

I didn't think it would come to this, but I can think of nothing else at the moment. I pull out my checkbook and write a check for ten thousand dollars. I can do it. I've had a good year. I should let Tomás finish Wally off, however much it would hurt Alice, but I can't since I promised her I would do my best to help him.

Tomás looks at the check, then tucks it into his pocket.

"Leave," he says. "Don't come back. Or I'll kill him. And I'll have every right."

I help Wally up. He's doubled over. His clavicle is broken. His left arm, which lies limp, turns inward at an odd angle. He winces with every step and breathes strangely.

That night at the hospital, I tell a nurse he's fallen awkwardly against a curb. It seems plausible, and they don't ask other questions. Wally looks like an old dog lying on the stretcher, and I leave before the examination is done.

Then we don't see him for five or six years. A few months before he turns up again, I read that Maria Rodriguez has won a national award for her poetry, which, as a junior in college, she's already collected into a book for a major publisher. There are claims she's plagiarized. Articles cite other young people who notoriously stole from earlier writers, but no one comes forward with proof about Maria.

Then one evening, suddenly finding Wally on my doorstep, I wonder if Maria's fame is related to his visit.

He's lost weight. His mustache has gone gray. He's been working as a roofer on condos somewhere near Vegas. He asks for Alice, and I let him in. She hasn't yet told me about the two of them as teenagers.

I take a walk to give them privacy, and by the time I return, Wally is gone. Alice is standing on our porch, looking out at the thick bougainvilleas surrounding our house. I can barely see her face in the dark.

"He ask for money?" I say.

She shakes her head. "Don't be an asshole. He's broken."

"Broken or broke?"

"It's not like that. He was saying goodbye."

"He going to join the army?"

"I said don't be an asshole. He's my brother."

"You sure don't act like it," I say. Alice and I have been having money troubles. A few start-up ventures I invested in are doing poorly, and that threatens my plan to retire in ten years. So I'm being surly.

"He's going to Alaska if you have to know. A friend of his got him work on the North Slope, something to do with maintenance on the pipelines. I don't know. He just said he was going and probably wouldn't be back."

"Ever? We'll never see him again?" I crack a smile.

"Don't," Alice says.

"I know," I say. "He's your brother. I get it."

For weeks after that, we don't sleep in the same room.

△△△

About a year later, I received an envelope. Inside is a computer printout of an article about Maria. And there's a tiny slip of paper that says, Please come in person. The return address on the envelope is Tomás Rodriguez's.

And because I'm curious or feeling guilty, I go. I drive back to Wellston.

I use the old knocker in the shape of a fist, and Tomás answers the door. I expect him to be diminished by the years, but he's as robust as ever.

"Come in," he says.

We sit before the unlit fireplace in his den. It's a peaceful room with the amber light shining on the wooden bookcases. We sit in two leather chairs across from each other. He offers me a drink.

"No," I say. "I came to find out what you want."

He hands me a sheet of paper. "Part of me thought you'd have looked me up after that night."

"I didn't want to have anything to do with you. You did a good job scaring both of us off."

"I did," he agrees.

The paper is his rap sheet. I read it aloud. "Felony domestic violence. Aggravated assault. One month in FDC Houston."

"It should have been three to five years," he says. "I was playing then and making the most money of my career. The charges were in the off-season, and the judge was a big football fan. He locked me up for the summer. I was back in time for training camp, no fines from the NFL."

"I still don't get it."

"It was Maria's mother. Maria, of course, wasn't born then, but we were together a long while before we had her."

"And you fought?"

He smiles. "Fighting would imply it was an even match." He looked at his empty hand as if not pouring the drink had left some hole in how he'd seen this conversation going. "All I can say is I was an angry man. I got off on hurting people. The game makes you that way."

"Sounds like an excuse," I say.

"You're right, of course. We weren't particularly poor growing up. I didn't even have that chip on my shoulder. Not like my mother's people, who came up from Michoacán. They tapped pine resin for a turpentine manufacturer. Tough work. They had nothing. Me, I had it easy compared to them."

"What's this have to do with me?"

"You're able to see all sides," he says. "Or maybe it's because I took your money. Maybe I think that buys you an explanation."

"What if I don't want one?"

"You ever hear of a devil's bargain? Maybe your money buys you an explanation, whether you want it or not."

"I'll take that drink, then."

He smiles slightly. He pours us Blue Label, neat.

"Maybe your friend Wally deserves this more," he says. "That's what I want to say."

"Why?"

"He could see me for what I was."

I take a drink of the whiskey and wait out the silence. Tomás begins.

"The first time Wally came to the house, I'd been chopping wood and, on my way into the garage, I dropped the ax. It came down on my calf and took a little chunk of flesh. Nothing major, but I was bleeding like a stuck pig. It made me angry. I felt the old heat come back into my chest. I ranted, just howling and swearing, throwing tools, breaking a few pieces of antique furniture.

It'd been a while since I'd been that violent, but I let loose. Soon as I was finished, I walked out into the drive—panting—and Wally was standing on my porch chewing on a goddamn toothpick with a package in his hand. I hadn't heard him pull up. Cool as anything, he says, 'I need you to sign for this.'"

Tomás smiles fully. "That brother-in-law of yours has one shit-eating grin."

I raise my tumbler to that.

"You should know," he says, "he didn't start writing her letters until then. Yes, he'd been stealing hers, but we racked that up to terrible service. We even made a few complaints. I'm saying that he didn't write to her until after that day with the ax. "

"So, how is that important?" I say.

Tomás grew pensive and then said, "I think he was checking up on her after seeing me and my anger. I pieced this together after you guys showed up here. I made Maria tell me everything. She, of course, didn't know about my temper tantrum in the garage, but when she gave me a look at the letters, they were dated. I did the math myself."

"What did his letters say?"

"They ask after her. They also cross a line, yes. Declarations of love. But they aren't explicit. I see that now." He holds up a bundle of tri-folded letters. They've been sitting on a small table beside his chair all this time. "They're not predatory, I suppose."

He stands with the letters as if he's going to walk them to me and lay them in my lap. Then he leans down and sets them in the fireplace. He opens a sizeable antique tinderbox on the mantel and produces a fireplace match.

"Given the distance and a little time," he says, "I might even have appreciated what your brother-in-law had to say."

"You're going to burn the letters."

"I'm protecting my daughter."

"Like you did before."

"Not like before. One of the things you might be asking yourself is, why tell you this after seven years?"

"I guess you're going to get to that."

"I will, but first, you need some background."

"Why? Come to the point already." I'm chattering, trying to get to the part where we discuss why burning Wally's old letters will be a good thing. The letters are the last evidence of any crime Wally committed. They're about to go up in flames, which should thrill me. Considered alongside Wally's removal to Alaska, I should be ecstatic. But relief is never whole. I'm dying to read the letters. I'm dying to know why Tomás kept them for so long. Is there some explanation for what all of it means?

"My wife left me pretty soon after Maria was born. I was still a very angry man then. I thought it might help, moving here, somewhere remote. I picked it at random. A friend of mine hunted deer every year not far from here, and I came out with him once. When Maria's mother left me, I remembered how far away this place felt from everything. I'd saved enough to retire, live modestly, and still pay the alimony and child support."

"Again, what's the point?" I'm growing frustrated now. "Get to it!"

"I will, I will." He stares off into space and continues. "A year after she left me, Maria's mother was dead. Inflammatory breast cancer. Bones, lymph nodes, lungs, all within a few months. Maria was my second chance. I raised her right. I rebuilt myself into something serene."

"I appreciate that," I say. I think of my own failings as a father. "But how does that explain why I'm here?"

"Maria's letters to her grandmother were what connected her to her mother. She started writing as a way—I don't know—to reach beyond this place. Your brother-in-law stole that from her."

I stand up and approach the fireplace to try, casually, to lift the letters out, but Tomás holds out his left arm.

"You're not going to see them," he says. He lights a match and says, "I asked you here because my daughter's book came out. She sent me a copy. I recognized a great many of the lines immediately from these letters." He drops the match on the pages, and they flame. "I have to protect my daughter," he says. "You don't strike me as a litigious sort of man, but I can't let you see what he wrote. On the other hand, I wanted you to know he wasn't as bad as you might have thought.

"And if you try and tell anyone," Tomás says, "about what I've told you, I'll deny every bit of it."

Then he rises, and with the pages of Wally's old letters burning in the fireplace, he hands me a copy of Maria's book.

"So you understand," he says. "I forgive your brother-in-law."

△△△

One day, in our quiet house, I took down Maria's book from the shelf and read Alice a particular poem. I know that poetry doesn't count for much today, but in Maria's work, there's something people respond to. She has a following.

The poem I read that evening is about a blind man who has his sight miraculously restored. The miracle turns out to be an awful thing. The blind man weeps night after night. When his wife questions him, he explains that most of us can't get past the way we see ourselves; we can't imagine how amazing and beautiful and good we look to those who genuinely adore us. We can't understand we're better people than we'll ever know. By being able to see his own image in mirrors and windows and lakes, the blind man has lost the only version of himself that ever mattered, the one seen through his wife's eyes, which stood in for his own.

I try, fumblingly, to tell Alice that it pertains to her. If she could see herself as I see her, she'd understand all she's done for Wally. I add something unhelpful like, "So try not to beat yourself up about it."

That brings a smile, and she says, "Roger, I think what you're not seeing is that the poem pertains to you. I've never had trouble understanding myself as being loved."

She leaves it at that.

ΔΔΔ

Somewhere in Alaska near the North Slope is a corrugated steel building that houses equipment for oil rigs. The wind gathers the snow along the dark-blue outer wall in sheer white angles. Inside, a man is operating a forklift. He drinks some on especially cold nights, and he's known as a bit of a carouser. Yet there's something defeated about him. Maybe the scar running down through his thin hair, tobacco-stained mustache, or pale, sunken cheeks remind you he was once livelier and fuller-faced.

Nobody really knows who he is. He has the odd habit of trekking out into the snow some nights just to stand with his arms outstretched as if he could embrace the entire spotless horizon.

He is in his navy parka, the fur-trimmed hood, his breath rising like exhaust from a struggling piece of machinery. There he is, howling. Howling for someone to love. Someone that looks like Maria Rodriguez.

A BARISTA NAMED ASTRID

She was new at Starbucks, the place I got my coffee each morning. I've been going there for almost three years and this morning was the worse experience I've had there ever.

I didn't deserve such treatment from her. So why did she do it?

She, the barista, didn't smile back at me. And she was rude and grumpy. To top things off, she asked me to say my name three times, and still misspelled it on the cup.

If that wasn't enough, she rolled her eyes as she turned, and said something under her breath because I had ordered something unusual.

I can tell if my order is right by its color —a rich copper rust. What I received was the color of dirt.

Her name is Astrid, according to her name tag, which means divinely beautiful in Scandinavia. And she is gorgeous, almost like a movie star, but not today, not with her frown and attitude. And the spilled coffee on her ruffled front blouse.

She is definitely not having a good day. When she told me to "have a good day," after I paid, I felt she meant the polar opposite of that.

Should I tell on her? Do I speak to the manager perhaps and tell him or her about Astrid?

No, I won't. Why? Because today is 9/11. Perspective is important, about coffee and life.

Marcus Aurelius once wrote:

"Reject your sense of injury and the injury itself disappears."

My experience with Astrid pales in comparison to what others experienced on this same day.

MARGIE

The unthinkable had happened.

Her longest relationship—after the one that ended in her marriage, was kaput, over and done with, gone forever.

And it happened in the blink of an eye… a blink of *her* eye, Rebecca Collins, the vamp of Vista Verde, the senior community east of San Diego where she and Daniel lived.

Three months of her life wasted.

God must be punishing me for something, she thought, or He would not have done that to me.

Margie Simmons looked in the mirror and tried to find the flaws that would have changed Daniel's mind about her. She was not young, but youthful appearing for a woman of 62.

She worked out every other day in the gym with weights, walked for an hour along the hiking paths adjacent to Vista Verde, and watched her weight, keeping it to 130 to 135, the same as in high school. No problems there.

She looked closely at her face. She wasn't movie star beautiful, but she wasn't ugly either. "Fetching," was the word her late husband used to describe her, something he heard in a pirate movie once.

Leaning toward the mirror, she noticed her many fine lines and wrinkles. Yet, they didn't show as much from a few feet away because of her tan, which he she kept year round in the tanning salons nearby.

She smiled. No problem there. She'd spent a small fortune to get a nice smile, something she'd hadn't while married to Bill when money was an issue.

So why did Daniel change his mind? He once mentioned that she looked like his first wife who he loved dearly, though she left him for another man. Maybe he was afraid she would do the same. Or, perhaps variety was what he was looking for.

She asked him why he preferred to date Rebecca instead, and he said he didn't know, he just did.

All that had happened a month ago. With no other real prospects she knew of, Margie decided to volunteer more. Perhaps her time was best spent doing something constructive instead of worrying over what could have been with Daniel.

That's why she was present that Thursday night in June when Margie learned a newcomer, Roger, volunteered the same night at the Family History Center. One look at him and she knew she was interested, but would he interested in her?

And what about the third person involved? God. He had to be agreeable as well.

That night she was sure God hung about the large one-room building behind the parking lot of the Church of Latter-Day Saints and listened in on their conversation from the dark corner dedicated to microfilm research.

During the school year, when his grandkids were around, Roger volunteered in the mornings, and this was his first evening at the center. During the two years since he'd retired to this town, Roger and Margie had taken notice of each other at church and organizational meetings, but they had never been together in an intimate setting like this.

That's what it felt like to the two of them, that the Heavenly Father was watching their every move and nudging them toward each other. There was a sense of urgency in the air, even though it was only eight o'clock, two more hours to go until closing time, and only one hobbyist genealogist still in the building, slowly scrolling his way through miles of microfilm in search of his forebears.

"Would you like some hot chocolate? I'm thinking of making some," Margie said to Roger. They had been sitting across from each other at an oval table in the middle of the room, Roger at the computer, processing information requests coming over email, and Margie filling out loan forms and coloring in the volunteer shift schedules for the next month.

"No, thank you. I don't really like chocolate."

"Lucky you! For me, one of the hardest things about joining the Church was having to give up all of that, tea, coffee, you know."

"Lifelong habits are hard to break. I've tried the stuff, but it's never appealed to me."

"This reminds me of my mother, when she was dying. I brought her a cup of coffee, and she refused it, she said she never really liked the taste of it. This was a woman who'd made a pot of coffee first thing in the morning every day of her life! She always made it for my father and never drank it herself. Imagine that."

"People without faith choose strange things to believe in."

Margie had lost her mother three years earlier, and Roger not only had outlived his parents but he had also, more than a decade ago, buried his wife. Now, Margie at sixty-two and certainly Roger at seventy-one were the next in line.

Roger rode his bicycle for exercise, and Margie ate at least one apple every day, cut it up into pieces and packed it in her purse, in a plastic baggie, to snack on throughout the day.

They both went to church regularly, Roger a lifelong Mormon, and Margie a convert after her ugly divorce fifteen years ago. And yet faith did not make the idea of death comforting or even approachable. Instead of picturing a meeting with the Heavenly Father, Margie kept stubbornly coming back to the memory of her mother's deathbed, the image of sunken eyes and immobile hands lying on top of the bedsheets.

Roger always believed that families were forever, that if he was valiant in his devotion to the Church, after death he would be reunited with everyone he loved. But now that his wife was dead, Roger was living on his own and enjoying it very much; he felt like a schoolboy at the beginning of summer vacation.

"Listen to this," Roger said. "Here somebody thinks she's related to Boleslaw the Brave, the first king of Poland."

"Everyone's related to Charlemagne, but Boleslaw? What a name!"

"Maybe we could use him for our trivia contest." Margie pushed aside her requisition forms and reached for the office laptop. She situated the screen to touch the back of the monitor of the computer Roger was using, and pulled up Wikipedia. "Boleslaw the Brave," she read, "born in 967 AD, one of the most powerful monarchs in eastern Europe, brought Christianity to Prussia—"

"A good guy, then?"

"I've always wondered what Prussia was."

The building housing the Family History Center wasn't much: a single room, partitioned into an open study area, a nook with a few shelves of reference books and microfilm stacks, and an adjacent dark area with several microfilm-viewing machines, where their one remaining visitor that night pored over old records.

The wooden table in the middle of the room, where Margie and Roger were sitting, was lit by two desk lamps and the glow of their computer screens. The overhead light was off—Margie liked it that way. She complained that overhead lamps were too bright and made the space seem like an emergency room.

The information requests Roger was processing were of an entirely trivial nature. How late is the center open on Saturdays? Can I register for the class on reading gothic German script, even though the website says the class is already full? Who's the expert on English family history, and when can I see her? Roger was going a mile a minute answering these questions.

"Old Prussians were conquered and completely vanquished by the Teutonic Knights," Margie read. "Isn't Wikipedia great? It's got answers to every question I can think of!"

"No wonder the Prussians were vanquished," Roger said. "I mean, if their religion was paganism."

"But the Teutonic Knights, there's an ambitious crowd. They united with something called the Han-se-atic League, and took over the entire Baltic region. Not bad, right?" Margie said sardonically.

"They didn't have those cruises going around the Baltic back then, did they? You and I should take a trip, visit all those countries. Germany, Sweden, you know," replied Roger, equally sardonic.

Roger had traveled this route as a young man, after he'd completed his mission to Europe. In Norway he had met his future wife, a recent convert to the Church, and proposed to her on the eve of his return to the United States. These memories were so blurry, they had stopped being true memories a long time ago, becoming family legends, the stories they told their children and grandchildren during holidays. But the physical experience of travel, and particularly the discomforts of it—the cold and wet breeze on the deck of a cruise ship, the unpleasant sour smell of the water—this he remembered well, and found that he thought of it with sadistic longing.

"You would enjoy taking a cruise. A perfect day on a ship can make it seem like you're going to live forever," Roger said. Expressed out loud, the thought sounded heretical, and yet the romance of the idea was so strong, Roger did not want to give it up. "Maybe I'll have that cup of hot cocoa after all."

"Do Teutonic Knights still exist?" Margie said. "I would like to be one. Bring Christianity to remote lands, fight the good fight."

In her previous life, Margie had been a nurse anesthetist, working in hospitals for more than forty-five years before she retired. She had long been inured to the everyday gore of disease and dying. She had seen it all—especially back in the 1960s, when she and her husband lived in Texas and she was the only person in three counties to deliver anesthesia during surgery. Caring for her mother through the months of her slow decline wasn't particularly unusual in terms of the physical experience, but Margie found herself unprepared to deal with the emotional turmoil of it, with her inability to express her fear and loneliness to a single human being. She had been long divorced by then, and her children and their families lived far away, and in any case she had never been one to burden others with her emotional baggage. Even in church she did not feel comfortable speaking out and sharing her experience with others—she didn't want to sound as if she was complaining.

"I'm hungry," Roger said. He yawned and stretched his torso, straightening his posture in the chair. "It's amazing how hungry you can get sitting all day."

A cell phone went off in a digital version of the old-fashioned telephone ring. God was watching Margie and Roger, but others had their priorities as well. Margie rolled her eyes but dug the phone out from the depths of her purse and picked up on the third ring. "Yes, hello," she said. She spoke quietly in order not to disturb their visitor in the microfilm room but loud enough for Roger to hear every word. Roger tried to give her some privacy by burying his head in the computer but was curious and listened. He was glad to hear her voice acquire a sharp edge as she spoke to the stranger. "I can't meet you tonight, I'm working the late shift here at the center. I'm not sure what I'm doing this weekend. How about I call you back?"

She hung up and hid her phone away with a deep sigh. Roger cleared his throat. "A man wants to date me," she said.

"And you? Do you want to date him?"

"Well, me, I just want to be friends. The whole thing is a nuisance. He wants to take me out to dinner, but I would much rather stay home and cook for myself. I am not much for going out."

"Is he in the Church?"

"This guy? Yes, he is. You probably know him. My kids keep trying to set me up, if you can imagine. One of my daughters even tried to get me to do online dating. She set up a profile for me on LDS Singles. But I think I'm too old for that."

Margie didn't feel old. In fact, sitting across from Roger and watching the blush take hold of Roger's pale, clean-shaven cheeks, she didn't feel her age at all. She could've been fifteen or a hundred, it wasn't her physical age that mattered but the fact that here was a man whose spirit seemed to be completely in tune with her own. Roger had the same sensation—as if a communication was occurring between them that went beyond words, one that could never have been contained by the sounds that escaped their mouths. Human language, he thought, was not adequate for spiritual union.

"Boy, I'm hungry," Roger said, patting himself on the stomach.

"I found a candy bar in my purse earlier today," Margie said. "I don't usually eat candy, and I don't have any idea where it came from, but it's packaged and sealed. Would you like to have it?"

The room grew quiet, as if God was holding his breath. They could hear the gentle whirring of the fans inside their computers. The clock above the bathroom door ticked audibly. There were no windows in the small library, but the walls were paper-thin, and they could hear a car leaving the church parking lot. Roger thought he heard the shuffle of the microfilm being rewound in the dark room and remembered that they still had a visitor in there. Margie glanced at the laptop, where the page about the Teutonic Knights was still open.

"Would you like to close this place early tonight?" Margie said. She felt her heart skip a beat and then come back aflutter. She was tempted to grab her left wrist and measure her pulse.

"I've answered 109 emails today. Not bad for one evening's work, huh?" Roger replied quickly. Margie's question sounded very much like a proposition, which made him feel excited and scared at once. He asked cautiously: "What do you have in mind?"

"Whole Foods is still open, you could get a sandwich there—or a salad, they have wonderful salads. Although it's a dangerous place. The other day I went there to buy a loaf of bread, and they had fresh strawberries on sale. I ended up with a box of them—and whatever am I going to do with a whole box of strawberries?"

"So, what are you going to do? I mean, tonight? Are you hungry?" Roger asked. Neither of them was working anymore, but they kept their eyes buried safely in the screens of their computers, both too shy to meet the other's glance. This sudden shyness scared Margie and made her physically uncomfortable. To hide her embarrassment, Margie closed her laptop and picked up the pile of papers she'd left unfinished before.

"Oh, I don't know. I have a sandwich waiting for me at home," she said.

It was maybe at this point, or maybe a few moments earlier, when Roger had been hesitating about which question to ask, that God quietly slipped out of the building. The room grew silent again, but this time the silence was peaceful, allowing Margie and Roger to restore their breathing.

Roger could hear his stomach growling, and he was starting to feel light-headed. Usually he kept a very regular schedule for his meals, and it had been a long time since he'd had to work through dinner, so he hadn't thought of packing a snack. Margie remembered a phone call she owed her daughter; she had been meaning to call her tonight, from the center, during one of her breaks. Her daughter lived in New York, three time zones away, and now it was too late.

"Do you want to tell our visitor we want to close by nine?" Roger said.

"Sure, but you do it. I'm too shy!"

"Me too! I too am very shy." Roger grinned and got up from his seat. He placed his hands on his hips and stretched his torso forward and backward, cracking his joints. "Boy, this feels good."

Margie got up and, following his lead, stretched, lifting her arms up and then trying to touch her toes. Together they walked around the copy machine to the entrance of the microfilm-reading area, and Roger announced, loudly: "The center will be closing in fifteen minutes—please finish up—"

He interrupted himself in the middle of the phrase, because he and Margie saw at the same time that all the machines were switched off, the microfilm rolls had been put away, and the room stood empty, as if there had never been anyone there at all.

SAYING GOODBYE

'My name is Mathew, and I'm an alcoholic.' He said that at the first meeting of A.A. I attended.

We met at the break and became friends right then. 'Why?' I asked him later.

'Because,' he said, 'you look like you need a friend, and I saw myself in you at my first meeting, ready to make a mistake and walk out of here.'

I struggled with my own introduction, of opening up for the first time about my disease, and saying it in such a public way at the meeting.

'I'll help you with that,' he told me. And he did. He had me rehearse in front of him dozens of times, until I no longer felt ashamed of what I was doing.

Today, I'm not here today just to remember a friend, I'm here to say good-bye to a part of myself. Mathew was that, and much, much more.

ABOUT THE AUTHOR

John Corral

He is an award-winning author of mysteries, thrillers, suspense, legal dramas, and westerns. He also co-wrote and edited women's stories of love and life with Tanya Angel, and contributed and edited poetry with Ian Lewis and Iris Mede.

Books by the author include THE RED LION FISH PARADOX, WATERCOLOR EYES, THE SAD PICNIC, SERIAL SINS OF SIBERIA, END OF THE PIER, THE COLORS OF LOVE, LIFE, AND DEATH, LUST, LIES, AND LOVE, GETTING SADDAM'S GOLD, LOVE TIMES ELEVEN, THE GRISLY EFFECTS OF GREEN, DID HOLLYWOOD CAUSE THE CUBAN MISSILE CRISIS?, HIS FINAL RESTING PLACE: ELVIS, REDHEADS ARE RELENTLESS, DELPHINA: VOODOO QUEEN, 30 FLASHES OF FICTION, 15 FLASHES OF FICTION, 15 MORE FLASHES OF FICTION, MYSTERY AND MALICE, IMPERFECT KILLING, PROSECUTION MISCONDUCT, REMEMBERING DIXIE, BEYOND THERE BE DRAGONS and THE MOST DANGEROUS MAN IN THE WORLD.

Books with Tanya Angel include PARIS STREET STORIES, THE SECRET LIVES OF SMILES, THE DUCHESS, WHERE THE HEART IS, and WHEN THE HEART LAUGHS IT SHOWW AND WHEN IT DOESN'T IT SHOWS EVEN MORE.

Books with Ian Lewis and Iris Mede include FLOWING LIQUID LIFE, DREAMS OF A PERPETUAL DREAMER, EVOLVING LOVE, LET LOVE FLOAT, ORDINARY LIVES EXTRAORDINARY LOVES, LET LOVE LEAD THE WAY, REAL PASSIONS REAL LOVE, LOVE THAT CHANGES EVERYTHING, THE SENSE OF SORROWS PAST, LOVE DEVILISH LOVE DIVINE, TALKING DIRTY ABOUT DESIRE, LOVE WORTH REMEMBERING, THE PLEASURES AND PAIN OF LOVE, WHEN LOVE LIFTS YOU HIGH, and WHEN LOVE SIZZLES.

John is also the author of TWO BROTHERS, a western, 3 LIFE LESSONS, an essay, and SEEING YOU, a book of poetry.

9 798826 311011